KU-631-765

Books in the Riley Bloom series

Radiance

Shimmer

Look out for

Dreamland

For older readers

The Immortals series

Evermore

Blue Moon

Shadowland

Dark Flame

Night Star

Everlasting

www.AlysonNoel.co.uk

SHIMMER

A Riley Bloom Novel

Alyson Noël is the author of many books for teens, including the bestselling The Immortals series. Her books have been published in thirty-five countries and have sold millions of copies around the world. She lives in California, where she's busy working on her next novel, but her favourite city is Paris. If Alyson could travel back in time she'd visit Renaissance Florence, but only if she could take her modern-day grooming habits! Alyson is an eternal optimist, who always believes in silver linings.

SHIMMER

A Riley Bloom Novel

Alyson Noël

MACMILLAN

First published in the US 2011 by Square Fish, an imprint of Macmillan

This edition published in the UK 2011 by Macmillan Children's Books
a division of Macmillan Publishers Limited
20 New Wharf Road, London N1 9RR
Basingstoke and Oxford
Associated companies throughout the world
www.panmacmillan.com

ISBN 978-0-330-53038-5

1 3 5 7 9 8 6 4 2

A CIP catalogue record for this book is available from
the British Library.

Printed and bound in the UK by CPI Mackays, Chatham ME5 8TD

For my mom, for everything!

*"Forgiveness is the fragrance the violet
sheds on the heel that has crushed it."*

—mark twain

If you think you know what it's like to be dead—if you think it's just an eternity of harp music and cloud lounging—well, think again.

Ever hear the saying, Life goes on?

It does.

Long past the point when everyone else thinks it stopped.

Take it from me, I've been dead for just over a year, and from the moment I crossed that bridge to the other side—well, that's when things really got interesting. . . .

I

"Go on, Buttercup—go get it, boy!"

I cupped my hands around my mouth and squinted into a blanket of gooey, white haze still hours away from being burned off by the sun. Gazing upon a beach that was just the way I liked it—foggy, cold, a tiny bit spooky even. Reminding me of our old family visits to the Oregon Coast—the kind I sometimes tried to re-create on my own.

But despite the infinite manifesting possibilities of the Here & Now, something about it just wasn't the same. Sure, you could replicate similar sensations, the way the tiny, pebbly grains wedged between your toes, the way the cool ocean spray felt upon your face, but still, it didn't quite cut it.

Couldn't quite live up to the real thing.

And clearly Buttercup agreed.

He sprinted after the stick, running headfirst into a

dad enjoying an early morning stroll with his son, before emerging on their other side. Causing the kid to stop and stare and gaze all around—sensing the disturbance, the sudden change in atmosphere, the burst of cold air—the usual signs a ghost is present.

The usual signs kids always tune in to, and their parents always miss.

I shut my eyes tightly, concentrating on mingling my energy with my surroundings. Summoning the vibration of the sand—the seashells—even the haze—longing to experience it in the same way I used to, knowing I'd have only a few moments of this before Buttercup returned, dropped the wet, slobbery stick at my feet, and we repeated the sequence again.

He was tireless. True to his breed, he'd happily *retrieve* for hours on end. A nice, long game of fetch making the list of his top-five favorite things, ranking right up there with dog biscuits, a warm patch of sun, bird chasing, and of course, his newest love—*flying*.

Nudging my leg with his nose, letting me know he was back, he stared up at me with those big brown eyes, practically begging me to hurl the stick even farther this time.

So I did.

Watching as it soared high into the sky before it pierced

the filmy, white veil and was gone. Buttercup dashing behind it, tongue lolling out the side of his mouth, tail wagging crazily from side to side—the furry, yellow tip the last thing I saw before the mist swallowed him whole and he vanished from sight. Leaving only a faint echo of excited barks trailing behind.

I turned my attention to the small flock of seagulls circling overhead, swooping toward the water and filling their beaks with unsuspecting fish, before taking flight again. Vaguely aware of the minutes slipping past with still no sign of him, I called out his name, then chased it with a spot-on imitation of my dad's special whistle that never failed to bring Buttercup home. My feet carving into the sand, leaving no trace of footprints, as I pushed through a fog so thick, so viscous, it reminded me of the time I'd flown through a cloud storm for fun, only to realize it was anything but. And I was just about to venture into the freezing cold water, knowing of his fondness for swimming, when I heard a deep, unmistakable growl that immediately set me on edge.

Buttercup rarely growled.

He was far too good-natured for that.

So when he did, it was safe to assume he'd stumbled upon something serious.

Something very, very bad.

I followed the sound of it. That low, gravely rumble growing in intensity the closer I crept. Only to be replaced with something much worse—a horrible snarl, a high-pitched yelp, and a sickening silence that made my gut dance.

"Buttercup?" I called, my voice so shaky, so unsteady, I was forced to clear my throat and try again. "Buttercup—*where are you*? This isn't funny, you know! You better show yourself *now*, or you will *not* be flying home!"

The second the threat was out, I heard him. Paws beating against the hard, wet sand, his quick panting breath getting louder and louder the closer he came.

I sighed with relief and sank down to the ground. Readying myself for the big, slobbery apology hug that soon would be mine, only to watch in absolute horror as the fog split wide open and a large dog jumped out.

A dog that *wasn't* Buttercup.

It was—*something else entirely*.

Big—the size of a pony.

Black—its coat matted and gnarled.

With paws the size of hooves that came hurtling toward me, as I screamed long and loud, desperate to get out of its way.

But it was too late.

No matter how fast I moved—it wasn't fast enough.

There was no escaping the chains of its sharply barbed collar that clanged ominously.

No escaping the menacing glow of those deep yellow eyes with the laser-hot gaze that burned right into mine, right into my soul. . . .

2

I curled into a ball, pressed my nose against my knees, and covered my face as I waited for the impact.

Waited for the push of those paws, the bite of those razor-sharp teeth, the heat of that ominous gaze to sear straight into the heart of me.

But nothing came.

And, really, why would it when there was one major thing saving me from his attack?

One major thing saving me from *any* attack.

One major thing that I still hadn't grown used to—or at least not when I was in the middle of being scared witless.

The fact that I was dead.

Dead as a doornail.

Dead and buried.

Dead as . . . well, pretty much as dead as it gets.

The irony being that while I might have felt more alive than ever, the truth was that my physical body had died just over a year ago. Leaving me with this new, light and filmy, somewhat translucent version that looked an awful lot like the original, gravity-bound version, except for the fact that things could easily pass through me now, whereas they couldn't before.

Things like oversize hellhounds with matted black fur and deep menacing growls, for instance.

And, as luck would have it, I'd failed to remember any of that until Bodhi had already caught up with me.

Or, rather, make that Bodhi *and* Buttercup, my sweet yellow Lab, who's not only known me for almost all of my life, but who died in the car accident right alongside me, which, all things considered, you'd think would result in some serious loyalty.

But *noooo*.

There were no loyalties where Buttercup was concerned. He was all too eager to sniff and lick the fingers of just about anyone willing to pet him, feed him, or play fetch with him—including my ghost guide Bodhi. And as Bodhi laughed himself silly at the way I cowered on the sand, all coiled up into my own tiny, blond, ghost-girl ball of fear, Buttercup barked and drooled and tail wagged happily beside him, carrying on in a way that seriously made me rethink *my* loyalty to *him*, and pretty much had me hating Bodhi as much as I did the first time we met.

The first time he pushed me (literally!) into that awful room, where I was forced to undergo a super embarrassing, completely agonizing life review.

A super-embarrassing, completely agonizing life review, in which I also discovered that my whole entire existence, my brief twelve years on the earth plane, had amounted to little more than a joke—and that the joke was on me.

The whole thing had been a wash.

A waste.

A decade-long exercise in trying to emulate my older sister Ever in hopes of being just like her.

Only to result in some seriously ridiculous, seriously bratty, seriously stalkinglike behavior that, in the end, was pretty much impossible to defend.

A super-embarrassing, completely agonizing life review presided over by various members of the Council who informed me that based on the amount of time I'd lingered on the earth plane—stubbornly refusing to cross the bridge to the Here & Now in order to stay behind and spy on my sister, celebrities, former teachers, and friends (along with anyone else who might prove interesting but was otherwise unsuspecting)—I had a job to fulfill, one where I was expected to "coax and convince" lingering spirits to cross the bridge to their new hon

you will. And even worse, I'c

teacher/coach/counselor/boss (

likes to describe himself), who

answer to, but maybe even learn

Despite the fact that he no lo   .. big

dork he did then, despite the fact   .. a swapped the

nerd wear for some much cooler clothes, despite the fact
that he'd let his hair go all shaggy and loose to the point
where it curved down into his face in that cool guy, slightly
windswept, effortless way, despite the fact that every time I
looked into his brilliant blue eyes I was totally reminded of
the Zac Effron poster that used to hang on my old bedroom
wall, it still didn't make it okay for him to laugh at me the
way he did.

I continued to lie there, every single part of me just
wishing he'd stop and move on already. But when it became clear that he wouldn't, when it became clear that he
was trying to calm down just enough, to catch his breath
just enough, so that he could make the switch from laughing at me to making fun of me verbally, I jumped to my
feet. I straightened my white cotton dress that, in my haste,
had gotten all twisted around, tugged on the straps of the
pink and turquoise swimsuit I wore underneath, and
glared at him as I said, "Yeah, yeah, laugh all you want."

head and scowled, first at him, then at Butter-
who promptly lowered his head, tucked his tail
between his legs, and gazed up at me with those big brown
eyes that were impossible to resist. "But I'm telling you, if
you'd seen what I'd seen . . . well . . ." I shook my head and
made my mouth go all tight and grim, forcing the words
between gritted teeth, "I know for a fact you would've
screamed too."

I was ready for a fight, ready for some more of that not
entirely good-natured ribbing, when instead he just placed
his hand on my shoulder and peered at me in this highly
serious way that he had.

"I did scream." His gaze locked on mine. "But instead of
the stop, drop, and roll action that you just did, I ran like
the wind."

I narrowed my eyes and shrugged myself out from under
his grip. Not quite sure what he was getting at, and still not
convinced he wasn't trying to poke a little fun at my ex-
pense.

"It was back in England, in Devon, if I remember correctly." He squinted as though trying to remember the exact
date, like it'd been centuries ago or something, when we
both knew he kicked it just over a decade ago, back in 1999,
courtesy of bone cancer, and just days away from the mil-
lennium too. Then lifting his shoulders, he added, "Anyway,

they're most often seen in Devon, Norfolk, Suffolk, and Essex, but still, I—"

"Wait—what do you mean, *they*?" I asked, aware of Buttercup creeping toward my side, nuzzling my leg in a desperate attempt to ease his way back into my good graces. "You mean there's more than one?"

"Snarly Yows?" Bodhi tilted his head in a way that caused his bangs to swoop into his eyes. "Yeah, lots more." He nodded, combing his fingers through his hair and pushing the strands back into place.

"Snarly—*what*?" My voice squeaked, unable to make sense of the word.

"Snarly Yow, Black Shuck, Phantom Dog, Galleytrot, Shug·Monkey, Hateful Thing, Hell Beast . . ." He shrugged, instantly manifesting a long green straw he started to chew, as he looked all around. Face arranged as though he expected to find a whole pack of them storming the sand, but coming away with little more than a heavy shroud of mist, he just looked at me and said, "They go by a lot of different names. And though the legends slightly differ, when you get right down to it, it all amounts to basically the same thing. A big, black, menacing dog with glowing eyes—sometimes one in the middle of his forehead, sometimes where his head would've been if it weren't missing—" He looked at me. "That sort of thing. Though they're not relegated to just England. Once, while I was on assignment in Egypt, I spotted a really big one, much bigger than the one you just saw. I mean it was *fierce*. I thought for sure it was some kind of crazed black stallion. You can't even imagine the size of that thing." He shook his head at the memory. "Anyway, it was guarding some centuries-old tomb. That's what they like to do, you know—guard old graves and tombs and such."

He peered at me from under a thick set of lashes, lashes he probably enhanced in some way in order to make himself appear irresistible. From what I saw at graduation—or whatever they call that day when he first started to glow in that deep greenish shade that was enough to signal to whoever was in charge of these things that he was ready to serve as my guide—from all the catcalls and wolf whistles that followed him right from his seat all the way down to the stage, well, it clearly was working.

Or at least on some less-discerning spirits anyway.

Me, I was pretty much immune to it.

He continued to look at me, practically begging for me to be impressed with his exotic journey. But no way would I give that to him. No way would I give him the satisfaction.

So he'd traveled to Egypt. On assignment. Where he'd faced down some phantom dog that was even bigger than the one I just saw.

Big deal.

So what?

In the short amount of time since I'd crossed the bridge to my new home in the Here & Now, I'd already aced an *assignment* at a pretty impressive castle in the English countryside, had already soared directly above the bustling streets of London, and was at that very moment enjoying a nice little *vacay* on one of the Virgin Islands—all of that happening within a *very* short, *very* brief, amount of time, *thankyouverymuch*. Which left me with no doubt that there'd be plenty more travel in store for me, what with all the assignments I'd have, and all the lingering souls I'd be expected to cross over.

"Anyway," he said, still chomping away, that green straw bobbing up and down in his mouth in what was clearly an annoying habit held over from his time on the earth plane. "Even though legend says that coming across one is a bad omen—a portent of death—"

"A *portent*?" I looked at him, my brow rising, convinced he was trying to show off again.

"An omen, a sign, a—"

"I *know* what it means." I rolled my eyes and waved it away, waved away his lame attempt to impress me, to lord his oh-so-big vocabulary over me.

"Anyway, the thing is," he continued, squinting as he

gazed up and down the mostly empty beach, "even though the legends all claim that whoever sees a Black Shuck will be dead within a year, that's obviously something you don't have to worry about. I mean, seeing as you're already dead and all . . ."

"So that's it, then?" I placed my hands on my hips and stared. "You're just gonna let this psycho, phantom, hellhound run amok, and basically terrorize all the people on the beach, and do nothing to stop it?"

He shrugged, obviously not nearly as alarmed by the prospect as I was. "Guess I don't really see the point," he said. "I mean, face it, Riley, the only one who seems to be terrorized by the dog is *you*."

I searched his face, searched for obvious signs (*portents!*) of mocking, but came up empty. So then I said, "What about Buttercup, then? What about that yelp that I heard? He sounded scared to death—so to speak."

But Bodhi just laughed. "Mad maybe, but definitely not scared. That was my bad. I caught his ball in midair and flew with it. He wasn't too pleased, but you got over it, didn't you, boy?" His voice grew all soft and mushy as he reached down to give Buttercup a good scratch between the ears. And it was all I could do not to cringe when I saw how quickly my dog abandoned my side in order to scooch back toward Bodhi's, where he sat, happily gazing at him, all drooly and goo-goo eyed.

"Besides, whatever lingering spirits you find here are to be left alone. *No matter what.* Just remember, if it's not assigned by the Council, then it's none of our business." His face grew all serious, wanting me to know just how much he meant it. Then assuming his job was done, assuming he'd waged the winning argument, he added, "So come on, what do you say we forget the beast, ditch this fogged-out beach, and go check out the town?"

I placed my hands on my hips and gazed into a mist that seemed as though it wasn't about to burn off anytime soon. Still, if you knew where to look, you'd find a few patchy bits here and there, and I took them to be a promise that a beautiful day might be in the works.

And even though we were there on vacation, even though this little trip was awarded to us by the Council for a job well done after crossing over some ghosts who'd been haunting a castle for way too long (ghosts that no other Soul Catcher had been able to move on, including Bodhi, until I came along)—even though Bodhi was nice enough to let me choose the place and didn't lodge even a single complaint when I picked St. John (the island my parents had honeymooned on, solely because I'd heard them talk about it so often, and so wistfully, I just had to seize the chance to see it for myself), even though we only had a little time left before we'd have to return to the Here & Now, appear before the Council, and get back to the business of our next assignment—even though I knew all of that—I still looked at him and said, "I'm not going anywhere till I convince that dog to move on."

3

"We can't do it. *You* can't do it," Bodhi said, and though I chose to ignore him, it's not like that stopped him. "Riley, did you not hear me? If the Council didn't assign it, it's none of our business."

He looked at me, shot me this long, hard, determined stare, but I chose to ignore that too.

Partly because I was already moving away from him, already making my way down the beach, headed in the same direction that the Hell Beast had run in.

And partly because I wasn't interested in listening to that kind of dissent, nor to any dissent. Not when I was so busy forming a plan.

"It's not like we can just go crossing over whomever we feel like, whenever we feel like. There are rules about these sorts of things, rules you're not even aware of. Besides, it's not like you'll find him anyway," Bodhi called out from behind me, his voice fading, the pitch growing weaker and weaker with each passing step I took. "Seriously, you're just wasting your time. They only show themselves when they *want* to be seen. And even then, it's usually only when they're trying to ward off some kind of threat or something."

I stopped.

Dug my toes deep into the wet, grainy sand and reconsidered my whole entire game plan.

I was headed the wrong way.

Instead of going in the same direction the beast had run, I should've been headed the way he'd come.

The same direction I'd originally been headed.

The same direction Buttercup and Bodhi had returned from.

Because if what Bodhi claimed was true, then there was something over there that the old Snarly Yow/Phantom Dog/ Hell Beast found worthy of guarding. And if I could just find what that was, then I could also find him.

So I turned, turned and headed right back to where Bodhi was standing. Noting the look of smug relief on his face, the way he nudged Buttercup with his knee, signaling that now that I'd caved in to his infinite wisdom, now that I'd finally come to my senses and seen his side of things, it was time for us to move on.

But I just kept going.

Just sailed right past him, as I pierced though the fog and he called out from behind me, yelling, "Riley! I'm *serious*. Why do you *still* find it so impossible to listen to me? I thought we were past this. I thought we had an *understanding*. I am the *guide*, and you"—he paused, searching for just the right word, one that would serve to get his point across, but hopefully not offend. His voice sure and confident the second he found it and said, "and you are the *apprentice*. Which means you can't go making up assignments—you are *not* a free agent! You can only get them from the Council or me. Riley! This is *not* a joke. I'm completely serious. What will it take to get you to *listen* to me? To *respect* me?"

It was a lot of words.

Quite a mouthful really.

But to me, they were just a whole bunch of consonants and vowels haphazardly strung together.

The only reason I'd heard any of it was because he'd decided to follow me. And as he rushed to keep up, he added, "You can't just *do* whatever you want, you know. There are rules, and regulations, and all it takes is just one ridiculously irrational move on your part to jeopardize everything I've worked so hard to build! It's my *job* to look after you. I'm *responsible* for you whether you like it or not. And yet, even though you're well aware of that, even though you know all too well how I just got back in good with the

Council after almost getting demoted and falling out of favor, you insist on doing this. Refusing to stop and consider how your reckless ideas might affect *me*. You just get some crazy idea about saving some Hell Beast that's probably not even on the Council's radar, and then you just dive in headfirst, without the slightest consideration as to how you're about to risk all my hard work! You have no idea what you're doing, no idea what the consequences are, or just how much I have to lose! Besides, little do you know, but just like people on the earth plane have destinies to fulfill, spirits *also* have destinies to fulfill. Not to mention a little something called *freewill*, which is something you have *no right* to interfere with. The ability to exercise one's freewill is an *imperative* part of a soul *realizing* its destiny! *And,* I hate to break it to ya, but for someone who didn't get their glow on until *very* recently, for someone whose *barely* there, pale green shimmer clearly marks you as a member of the level 1.5 team, you are neither *allowed* nor *authorized* to interfere in anyone's *destiny* or *fate* or *chosen path* or *freewill* unless *specifically* ordered to do so by either the Council or me! *Why* do you not understand this? *Why* do I have to keep explaining it to you?"

And that's when I turned. That's when I spun on my heel, looked him straight in the eye, and said, "As it just so happens, that's *exactly* what I'm doing right now."

He looked at me, his expression a little muddled, chaotic—a result of that hectic word deluge he'd spewed forth.

"I'm exercising *my* freewill. And though I may not be as well versed in the rule book as you, O Mighty Guide of Mine, I'm pretty dang sure *you* lack the authority to keep me from realizing *my* destiny."

Then, without waiting for a response, I was gone. Feet pushing hard into the sand, intent on keeping my progress steady and sure, choosing walking over flying since, in my experience anyway, flying in the fog isn't near as much fun as it might seem at first. The poor visibility makes for a pretty blah view.

Bodhi's voice continuing to haunt me as he hurled words like *stubborn, obstinate, headstrong, overly willful, misguided, irrational, impulsive*—none of them the least bit flattering, but all of them piercing through the fog and trailing right behind me nonetheless.

And just like before, they bore no lasting effect.

To me, it was just a bunch of bippidy blah blah.

I mean, maybe what he said was true.

Maybe it wasn't.

It was of no particular interest to me either way.

Because despite what Bodhi claimed about the rules, and the Council, and my own very long list of extremely flawed character traits, there was one thing I knew for absolute sure:

There were no accidents, coincidences, or random events.

The universe just didn't operate like that.

I'd seen that dog for a reason.

And I was determined to get to the bottom of it.

4

Although I couldn't say for sure how far I had walked—due to the intensity of the mist I could neither see behind me nor in front of me—I did know that I'd walked for enough for Bodhi's voice to completely fade into nothing.

Walked for so long I could no longer hear Buttercup's panting breath or excited barks.

Aside from the constant lull and sway of the sea lapping the shoreline, and the familiar, almost-plaintive, cry of the seagulls soaring overhead, I couldn't hear much of anything.

Couldn't see anything.

Couldn't hear anything.

Which probably explains why I was so surprised when I stumbled upon it.

And I do mean *stumbled*.

I'd been so intent on merging my energy with the sand,

the sea, the sky, and all the rest of my surroundings, so focused on merging my vibration with that of the physical world, that one moment I was just strolling along, more or less minding my own business, and the next I'd toppled right over, headfirst.

Yep, even in my ghostly form I could still get tripped up.

Even though it probably seems as though I should've just slipped right through it, the thing is, in the end, it all came down to energy. In order to make contact with something more solid, in order to experience the earth plane in the same way I used to, I had to draw upon its energy. And my being so focused on drawing upon the energy of just about everything around me . . . well, let's just say that's pretty much what did me in.

I screwed up my face, pushed my long blond bangs out of my eyes, and glared at the offending piece just before me.

Expecting to find some kind of jagged, water-carved beach rock, only to see that it wasn't a rock at all—or at least not the kind I'd assumed.

Somewhere along the way, the beach had managed to transition from a misty shroud of white sand and turquoise waters into a desolate, seemingly forgotten, fog-free, patchy-grass graveyard without my even noticing.

A seriously decrepit, seriously *old* graveyard.

The kind with crumbling tombstones, sunken graves,

and creepy-looking trees with cruel, leafless branches that hovered in such a way they looked as though they'd pluck you right off the ground and into their clutches.

The kind of graveyard you see in scary movies.

Only this was no movie, this was the real thing.

I squinted at the tombstone that'd tripped me, searching for a name, a date, something that might mean something to me or provide a clue of some kind. It was so old and crumbly, all I could make out was the vague outline of what might've been an angel's wing, but could've just as easily been something else entirely, along with a partial name and date that'd been etched away by the cruel hand of time.

I looked all around, seeing there were more—lots and lots of them. Some similar, some not, some with elaborate markings and angels and crosses and things, some not much more than a sad little stump.

And just as I remembered what Bodhi had said about the Phantom Dog's penchant for guarding graves and tombs and such, I saw it.

Not the dog.

Not—well, not anything substantial enough for me to really put a label on.

Let's just say, it was more of a shimmer.

A soft, pinkgold shimmer.

And I watched, mesmerized, pretty much spellbound really, as it twirled and danced and flitted and jumped. Bouncing lightly from the head of each grave, gracefully leaping from tree to tree, until it finally landed before me. Hovering in place as I scrambled to my feet and watched in amazement as that glowing ball of energy slowly stretched, and curved, and transformed itself into a pair of eyes, a nose, a mouth, and teeth—

Transformed itself into—*me*!

It was all there.

All of my features present and accounted for.

Lanky blond hair: Check.

Bright blue eyes: Yep.

Semi-stubby nose: Roger that.

Completely sunken chest: Um, unfortunately, yes.

Fussy, overly frilly dress, with way too many sparkles and bows: *Wha*—?

I was speechless.

Really and truly speechless.

My eyes darting all around, searching for Bodhi and Buttercup, wondering if they were somehow behind it, determined to freak me out, creep me out, and teach me a lesson about making up my own assignments.

But when I turned back to her, er, *me*, er, *it*, I started to get really annoyed by the dress. I mean, seriously, one frivolous accent would've been more than enough, but to add frills *and* lace *and* ruffles *and* bows *and* buttons that actually sparkled and shone, well, it clearly amounted to complete and total overkill.

Besides, anyone who knew me knew I wouldn't be caught dead (literally!) wearing a dress like that. So that meant either Bodhi was seriously determined to get back at me for ignoring his rules, or someone else, someone who obviously *didn't* know me at all, had made the mistake of seriously underestimating me.

"Sorry." She smiled, instantly transforming *my* features into ones that belonged to someone else, someone who was totally unrecognizable to me.

The hair became brown and curled instead of blond and limp, the eyes a deep hazel instead of bright blue, the nose long and elegant as opposed to, well, the way mine was built, and a chest that bloomed into something a little more substantial than the pathetically, sunken version I was stuck with.

A chest that bloomed in a way mine never would.

But for some strange reason, she chose to keep the dress, which, had it been me, would've been the very first thing I would've ditched.

"It's always good for a scare though. Which I guess is why it's just too good to resist." She laughed in a way that lit up her face, the sound of it light and melodic and, well, *tinkly* even. Though her gaze stayed the same, heavy and observing. "It's naughty of me, I know, but sometimes . . ." She gazed all around and, I mean, *all* around. Her head spinning in quick circles, her neck creasing and twisting in the most grotesque way as she wrapped her slim arms tightly around her impossibly tiny waist. "Well, sometimes I just can't help myself." She looked at me again, her head having rotated all the way back until it snapped into place. "But, seeing as you're dead like me, I'll play fair. I'll stop with the games. Oh, and please excuse my lack of manners. My name's Rebecca, by the way." She smiled and dipped deep down into what I immediately recognized as some old-school, ladylike curtsy. Bowing her head before me, and revealing an array of even more ribbons and bows that meandered their way down her back.

I hesitated, still a little shaken from the whole head-spinning display, and waiting to see what else she'd come up with, what else she had planned.

But when nothing more happened, when she chose to remain as the same, over-accessorized version of herself, I nodded slightly and said, "I'm Riley." Hoping that alone would suffice, since I had no intention to curtsy. Not then, not ever.

Only to hear her reply, "Riley?" She squinted, her eyes

becoming two tiny pinpricks, devoid of all light. "Why, excuse me for saying so, but isn't that a *boy's* name?" She tilted her head to the side and stared. Her eyes providing no clue to what her real thoughts might be. And strangely, unlike a lot of the other dead people I'd met before her, I was unable to hear them. Somehow she'd found a way to hide them from me.

"Do I *look* like a boy?" I responded, more than a little miffed by her comment, and wanting her to know she was treading on very thin, very shaky ground.

But she just pressed her lips together and shrugged daintily. Taking her own sweet time to reply, acting as though it was just too close to call. As though she was actually wavering between the two choices of male versus female.

I was about to walk away, deciding I'd had enough of her games, when she brought her hand to my shoulder and tapped.

Only once.

Light and quick.

Yet that was all it took to instantly transport me all the way back to my very first day of school.

Back to the skinny, scrawny, jeans-and-sweater-wearing version of me, sporting what could only be described as a very ill-advised pixie cut.

A very ill-advised pixie cut that seemed like a good idea

at the time (mostly because my sister Ever had gotten her hair cut short too), but that ultimately left everyone, both classmates and teachers, assuming I was a boy.

It was as though I'd gone back in time.

I watched as the series of crumbly, old grave markers magically transformed into a group of small desks, while the clump of tall, creepy trees, with the wide, hollowed out trunks and long spindly branches that reminded me of the gnarled old fingers on a storybook witch's hands, turned into chalkboards and easels.

The walls closing in all around me, keeping me, trapping me, until what had once been an old, forgotten, abandoned cemetery transformed into an exact replica of my kindergarten classroom. The scene playing out exactly as I remembered, complete with hysterically laughing, fellow five-year-olds, and an overly apologetic, red-faced teacher.

"Riley, I'm *so* sorry," Mrs. Patterson said, her shoulders lifting in embarrassment, as a spot of color burst forth on her cheeks.

But that was nothing compared to the way I *felt*.

Our first assignment of the day—just after pinning our name tags to our chests—was to line up in two separate groups: boys on one side, girls on the other. And according to my teacher, I'd already failed that particular task.

One glance at my androgynous clothes and super-short,

tomboyish haircut, and Mrs. Patterson had assumed the worst.

Assumed I was a *boy*.

"What with your . . . I just assumed that you . . ." Her hand fluttered before her, as her eyes searched for a distraction, some kind of escape.

And I stood before my giggling classmates, my eyes squinched and stinging, my throat hot and dry, experiencing the full brunt of what it means to be horribly humiliated for the very first time in my life.

I gazed at all the other girls, taking in a seemingly never-ending sea of curls, and braids and barrettes and ribbons, all of them dressed in varying shades of pink and purple and sky blue—not so unlike that bratty ghost-girl Rebecca—and one thing became clear, perfectly clear: I was pretty much the worst thing a person could be.

I was *different*.

I was someone who didn't fit in.

While I'd left my house just a little while before feeling nervous for sure, but mostly excited and good, fifteen minutes into it, I'd already been tagged as a freak.

I bolted from my place and made a run for the door. But unlike my real classroom, this door was locked.

So then I bolted toward the large windows, but they were locked too.

Leaving me with no choice but to gaze all around, searching for an exit, and struggling to settle myself as the horrible truth slowly crept upon me:

I was trapped.

Held hostage in a classroom full of giggling, mocking, sneering students, whose hysteria rose and swelled and became so contagious, even my teacher couldn't help but join in.

Even though I knew, on some small level, that this wasn't exactly real, that it hadn't actually gone down in quite that same way, it's not like it mattered. Deep down inside, all the way down to the very core of me, the very *soul* of me, the emotions were exactly the same as they were that day.

I felt embarrassed.

Humiliated.

And fearful, and stupid, and completely insecure.

But worst of all, I felt *angry*.

Angry at my classmates for making fun of me.

Angry at my teacher for joining in.

Angry at myself for my inability to blend, for not being like all the other girls, for not trying a little harder to fit in.

Surrounded by a chorus of laughter that threatened to swallow me completely, I railed against the walls, the doors, pounding harder and harder, until one laugh in particular stood out from the rest.

One, single, tinkly laugh that raised above all the others and lured me right out of that mess.

The classroom dissolved.

The teacher and students disappeared.

While the surrounding space continued to shimmer and shine as thick squares of ash rained down all around— drifting lazily as they made their descent, clinging briefly to my shoulders and feet before getting stirred up again. Transforming the scene into some kind of darkly glistening, sinister snow globe of sorts.

She stared at me, her face solemn, unforgiving, as her long slim fingers traipsed down the front of her ridiculous dress. Plucking at the folds of the big, wide, yellow bow that slashed right across her middle, she looked at me and said, "Hmmm, that seemed most unpleasant for you." And before I had enough time to react, she added, "In fact, that must've left you feeling *really* awful and angry now, *didn't it*?"

I lowered my head, gazing down past the swimsuit and cover-up I'd been wearing ever since I'd arrived on the island, gazing all the way down to my ash-smudged toes and bare feet. Struggling to compose myself, to regain my balance, my bearings, but the truth was that whole scene she'd just manifested on my behalf had left me miles past shaken.

While I had no doubt she was baiting me, trying to upset me, get me all riled up and angry, I had no idea why.

All I knew was that despite the abundance of sparkles and bows and curls, this was one little ghost girl who *wasn't* made of sugar and spice and everything nice.

On the contrary, I was pretty darn sure she was made of something much worse.

Rebecca had a dark side.

Possibly even a secret of some sort.

She'd been hanging around the earth plane for too long. So long she'd grown jaded and bored and, let's face it, mean in a way that proved just how much she desperately needed to be crossed over before she could get any worse.

But even though I knew all of that, when my eyes met hers, I also knew there was no way I could go it alone.

I'd stumbled in where I clearly didn't belong, and I had no idea how to get out of that mess.

5

Just as she had appeared, she disappeared.

In a flash of shimmering light that flitted its way across the graves until it vanished from sight.

Leaving me right back where I'd started, alone in that creepy graveyard with no sign of the psycho dog, no sign of the psycho girl, no sign of anything other than the long forgotten memory she'd so effectively unearthed.

The impression lingering, clinging, refusing to let go—stubbornly growing and stretching until that one isolated incident became so big, took up so much space in my head, it easily trumped everything else.

Including the version I knew to be true.

While my more logical mind should've easily reminded me that the embarrassing scene I'd relived was just a single brief episode that only occurred that one time, a single brief episode that certainly didn't mark me as an outcast forever—while it should've reminded me how I'd managed to rise above it soon after, to the point where just a few days later, two of my classmates, Sara and Emma, each took a pair of scissors to their own hair in an attempt to mimic my look (much to their parents' horror)—my logical mind didn't seem to be working that day.

My logical mind was taking a little *vacay* of its own, leaving me alone, defenseless, swarmed by those long-buried feelings of embarrassment, and confusion, and deep seething anger. And as I made my way out of that graveyard, I couldn't help but gaze all about, couldn't help but wish there was some kind of place in which to deposit those feelings—a sort of emotional dumping ground, if you will—so that I could leave them behind and spare myself the burden of having to lug them around.

My thoughts soon interrupted by the sight of Bodhi pushing his way through the fog that continued to hover and pulse its way around the perimeter. Approaching me with a glaring gaze that served as a perfect match for his steely tone when he said, "Okay, Riley. Now that you've had your *fun,* now that you've enjoyed your little act of *rebellion,* I'm *ordering* you to come with me." He leaned forward, peering at me in a way that made it seem as though his face and voice were in a heated competition to see which could come off as the sternest.

I glanced between Buttercup and him, wincing at the way my dog, feeding off Bodhi's energy, gazed at me with a look that could only be read as pity.

"Because in case you've forgotten, this was supposed to be a *vacation*. A nice little time-out so we could both relax, have some fun, and, yeah, maybe even get to know each other a little better so that I'll be able to guide you more effectively in the future. But the only thing I've learned so far is that you are even more stubborn than I first thought. I mean, when I tell you to—"

I stopped him right there, flashed a palm in surrender and said, "Okay, okay," as I quickly moved past him. More than a little eager to get out of that dark and creepy grave-yard and back into the fog—desperate to leave it all behind, both literally and figuratively, and get on with the rest of the day. "I'm ready to hit it, ready to check out the town now. I'm no longer interested in that psycho dog. Seriously," I added, still moving forward, mistaking his silence for skepticism, and wanting to convince him that my sudden change of heart was for real. Knowing all too well that the price for *not* convincing him would be a never-ending string of questions I had no intention of answering.

For more reasons than one, I wasn't about to reveal what I'd been through—or at least not quite so soon anyway. Not while I was still trying to make sense of it in my own head.

"You were right." I nodded, a little too vigorously, probably overdoing it, overstating it, but it's not like that stopped me. I'd made a mistake—a terrible, impulsive mistake. I'd misjudged my abilities, and even worse, I'd misjudged the seriousness of upsetting the Council. It was like a moment of temporary insanity, but I was over it. Completely over it. From this point on, I was determined to listen and do as I was told. I'd already put it behind me. I hoped Bodhi would too. "So what do you say we walk or fly our way out of here? Either way, it's up to you. It's all good as far as I'm concerned."

I stopped. Stopped talking. Stopped walking. Just stood there with my back turned toward him, reluctant to glance behind me and see where I'd been. But when my words were met by nothing more than a long, lingering silence, I whirled around to face him. Ready to say or do whatever it took to get out of that place, only to realize he hadn't heard a single thing I'd said.

Bodhi was preoccupied.

Paying me no attention whatsoever.

In fact, it was pretty much the opposite. He'd gotten all turned around and was headed off in an entirely different direction.

Moving away from me in order to race toward a really pretty dark-haired girl, with the traitorous Buttercup keeping sharp at his heels.

And though I called out Bodhi's name, over and over again, it bore no effect. Either he couldn't hear me, or he didn't want to hear me. All of his attention was claimed by the slim, petite figure crisscrossing through the snarl of trees.

All of his attention claimed by the swiftly moving girl whose long dark hair lifted and bounced and whirled all around her like a shiny black cape.

The girl whose lovely dark eyes glinted and flashed, whose gleaming smooth cheeks brightened and flushed, whose entire face lit up in a blend of joy and love and delighted expectation, as she turned and smiled and beckoned him closer with a curl of her fingers.

He called out to her, the words soft, breezy, just barely a whisper, but there was no mistaking it. No mistaking the tone, no mistaking the allusion of longing, of yearning, when Bodhi, halting, cried, *"Nicole—please—don't go. Wait for me!"*

His feet moving quickly, racing past clumps of dead grass, pressing through clusters of graves. Gaining on her, getting closer still, until she stopped beside a particularly gnarled old tree and shifted her gaze from Bodhi to me.

And that's when I saw it.

Saw what lay behind the petite and pretty facade.

Though I was the only one who saw it.

The reveal was meant solely for me.

Bodhi continued to see what he'd always seen, which was something else entirely.

And before I could call out to him, before I could catch up or warn him in some way, he was gone. Leaving me with no choice but to just stand there and watch as she lifted one delicate finger, and smiled as she tapped Bodhi's shoulder.

Only once.

Light and quick.

But that's all it took for the barrier to slam down all around him.

Slam down around—*everything*.

Leaving me with nothing but the wail of Buttercup's plaintive howls, the fading whisper of Bodhi's yearning pleas, and the horrible truth of what really just happened before me.

Rebecca.

Horrible, horrid, ghost-girl Rebecca.

With her glowing-eyed hellhound beside her—had tricked both my guide and my dog and stolen them from me.

6

I stood there, gaping at a space that looked nothing like it had just a moment ago—nothing like the space I'd just vacated.

Other than a few of the outlying trees and rocks and patchy clumps of dying sea grass, the rest of it, the inside bits, were now encased in a sort of glimmering glow.

It *shimmered*.

Not unlike the shimmer I saw before—the shimmer that had turned from a small bouncing ball of light into Rebecca the over-accessorized, mean, little ghost girl.

Only this shimmer was bigger.

Much bigger.

Like a big, shiny bubble that reached its way around until it had nearly encased the entire graveyard. The bottom part blending flush with the earth, while the walls and sides were so smooth and round and glossy, it was nearly impossible to look without squinting.

Like a mirror, it reflected everything outside of it, while obscuring the secrets inside.

Although I couldn't see past my own glaring reflection, I knew my guide and my dog were both trapped in the same way I'd been. And, if their experience was anything like mine—well, then they were both about to find themselves reliving their own personal version of hell.

I squinched my eyes till they were nearly shut and continued to stare at the bubble, searching my brain for answers, clues, anything Bodhi might've mentioned about a pretty dark-haired girl named Nicole, but came up empty.

The truth was, I didn't know much about Bodhi's time on the earth plane. Aside from when and how he'd died, aside from his claim that he was on his way to being a professional skateboarder, I was ashamed to admit I didn't know much of anything.

I knew nothing about where he came from, nothing about where he lived, who his parents were, his friends, if he had any siblings, and if he ever really missed his old life as much as I sometimes missed mine.

Though, I guess the amount of longing he held in his voice as he called out her name pretty much answered that last part.

He did miss her. A lot. That much was clear. But what I didn't know was *why* he missed her—who she was—what she might've meant to him.

I slumped down to the ground and continued to squint at the shiny globe before me. Wavering between feelings of deeply seated shame at being so self-centered I'd never even bothered to learn my guide's personal history—never even showed the slightest bit of interest in learning—and wondering just what it was I could do to break them out of that place.

How I could free them from Rebecca's world of pain.

What my next move might logically be.

The longer I pondered, the worse it got, as I allowed my imagination to take over. Running amok with visions of Bodhi undergoing all manner of humiliation and emotional torture (our being dead may have left us well past the point of physical torture, but it did nothing to boost our immunity against things like fear and dread, and other forms of self-induced psychological warfare), while Buttercup . . . well, I couldn't imagine him ever experiencing a bad day in what had amounted to an overly cushy, almost ridiculously indulgent, well-fed, well-cared-for, former life. But knowing Rebecca, she'd dig up something, and I had no doubt it would involve her laser-gazed, razor-toothed, Hell-Beast companion.

Call it intuition, call it what you will: Even though I had no sure way of knowing what might've been going on in there, I knew it was wrong.

Terribly, tragically wrong.

I also knew that *I'd* brought it on.

If I hadn't decided to go snooping around, if I hadn't decided to go against Bodhi's warnings and track down that stupid Snarly Yow, none of us would be in this predicament now.

I'd decided to exercise my *freewill* by sticking my stubby nose where it clearly didn't belong.

And now my guide and my dog were both trapped as a result.

I felt awful, guilty, and, truth be told, more than a little worried about how all of this would go over with the Council. I had no idea how they'd punish me, though I'd no doubt they would. And while Bodhi had tried to warn me against it, tried to warn me against doing the very thing I was so determined to do, I'd failed to listen. Making me solely responsible for getting us into the mess, which also made me solely responsible for getting us out.

But as worried as I was about what I might face once I returned to the Here & Now, at that moment, I had to push it aside for more pressing concerns. My guide and my dog were trapped, and I could no longer allow myself to sit there and do nothing about it. So I sprang to my feet, rushed toward that gleaming bubble, and hurled my body against it. Pounding my fists into the sides, railing at it with all of my might—but it was no use.

It was impenetrable.

Despite my best efforts, I hadn't left even the slightest sign of a dent.

Only one thing was sure:

Absolutely no one was allowed in or out without Rebecca's consent.

7

I shrank back, shrank away from it all. Feeling anxious, helpless, and woefully inadequate as I gazed all around. Wondering if there was something else I could do that wouldn't make it any worse than I already had.

I'd already called out their names—already alternately pleaded with and threatened Rebecca—and was quickly nearing the point of losing it to complete and total hysteria.

Was well on my way to becoming so desperate, I was actually considering making a trip back to the Here & Now so I could try to recruit some kind of backup team that might be willing to help out—when I heard it.

A slight, barely there, rustling kind of sound that seemed to emanate from everywhere and nowhere.

I turned, my face wary as I searched for the source. Watching as it slowly emerged from the shrubbery—a foot, a leg, a torso, a head—all of it coming forth to say, *"You are Riley?"*

His eyes bore into mine in a way that, well, had I still been required to breathe, let's just say, would've been the exact moment I held my breath until it swelled up into my cheeks.

Would've been the exact moment I held it for so long my face would've turned blue as my eyes threatened to pop from their sockets.

But, as it was, I just met his stare with one of my own. Trying to decipher the truth from fiction—unable to tell if what I was seeing before me was actually real.

Even though he wasn't the least bit familiar, even though the words that followed meant nothing to me, that didn't mean Rebecca wasn't in on it, or somehow behind it.

That didn't mean she hadn't sent him forth for the sole purpose of terrorizing me.

"How do you know my name?" I narrowed my eyes until they were slits.

"I am Kanta. *Prince* Kanta," he said, keeping his face soft and still. "And you, Riley Bloom, have nothing to fear. Or at least not from me anyway."

I pulled my shoulders back, straightened my spine, and tilted my chin in a way that I hoped would come off as far more confident and commanding than I might've seemed at first. Steadfastly holding his gaze as I said, "While that doesn't really answer my question, just so you know, I have nothing to fear from anyone. In case you haven't noticed, I'm dead."

He half smiled. Hinting at what could have been a dazzling display of large, slightly crooked, boxy white teeth, pink-tinged lips, and two very deep dimples that marked his smooth, dark skin—if only he hadn't dropped it so quickly. "As am I." He nodded, presenting the words in a manner that was regal, kind, and serious all at once. Then he bowed low before me, his shiny bald head dipping and lifting, as those deep, ebony eyes settled on mine. "Normally, I would allow time for a more formal introduction, but I'm hoping we can move past all of that and get down to the business at hand."

"What business?" My brow rose as I took note of the details: the impossibly high cheekbones, the wide nose, the full lips, the strong chin, and the well-muscled body with the ultra-broad shoulders clad in what clearly amounted to a disgusting pile of rags.

My eyes grazing over a stained-and-battered white shirt that was neatly tucked into a pair of dark, severely torn, threadbare trousers cut off and frayed at the knees, and I couldn't help but wonder just what kind of *prince* would go around looking like that. Why someone of nobility, royalty even, would possibly choose to dress so . . . *shabbily*.

Though I shouldn't have been so surprised, since it's not

like he was the only one. Out of all the ghosts I'd met so far, not one of them chose to step it up a notch, keep up with the changing times, or take the slightest bit of advantage of the wonderful gift of instant manifestation that pretty much allowed for an all-access pass to the closet of your wildest imagination.

All of the ghosts I'd met so far had (much to my disappointment) been willingly stuck in some kind of tragically unfashionable time warp, insisting on wearing the same types of clothes they were last seen in alive, no matter the date.

"I apologize if my humble appearance has startled you, or left you doubting my genuineness in some way." He immediately rid himself of the rags, manifesting an elaborately patterned, colorful tunic in their place. "I trust this look will not offend?"

I flushed, aware of the color rising to my cheeks as a look of embarrassment crept across my face. And I couldn't help but wonder when I would ever learn to think nicer thoughts now that pretty much everyone around me (well, everyone who was dead anyway) could hear them? Or, at the very least (and far more plausibly considering it was *me*), when would I finally learn how to shield them?

I started to apologize, feeling bad for what he'd heard, but I didn't get very far before he quickly waved it away. Lifting his hand and flashing one heavily calloused palm as he said, "There is no need. Nor time for that matter. Please allow me to get right to the point since this is a matter of the utmost urgency. Rebecca has trapped your good friend, yes?"

"What makes you say that?" I squinted, not sure I could trust him. Not convinced he could be of any real help.

"I am aware of *everything* that happens in these parts. *Every. Thing.* Including your name. I've been aware of *you* and your problem from the moment it started. Which also means, I know you are in need of my help."

I looked at him, part of me wanting to deny I even had a problem, mostly because I was a little creeped out.

Okay, maybe I was a lot creeped out. I mean, here he'd pretty much just jumped out of the bushes, appeared out of nowhere really, claiming to know *everything*—and since I couldn't hear his thoughts either, I had no way of knowing just what his motives might be.

But when I gazed into his kind and shining eyes, I realized that thought had come from the more paranoid part of me.

The more reasonable part knew I needed help.

Needed it, like, pronto to say the least.

I'd gotten myself into quite a mess—found myself in a situation so beyond me, I was left with no choice but to look for a solution outside of my own, admittedly meager, means.

I was far too lost and clueless to even try to go it alone.

And that's pretty much the only reason I decided to take the leap—decided to place all my trust in this odd, shabby stranger who claimed to be a prince, despite the pile of evidence to the contrary.

Allowing the more logical part of me to reign as I squared my shoulders, looked him straight in the eye, and said, "I do need your help. I really do. Not only does she have my friend, but she's got my dog too."

8

He regarded me carefully, his face solemn, eyes grave, his gaze sweeping mine as though giving it some majorly serious consideration.

Then, without another word, with no other signal than the slightest nod of his shiny bald head, he turned, motioned for me to follow, and led me right out of that graveyard, away from the bubble and over to what appeared to be a small, straw-covered hut on the sand.

I stood at the entrance, totally unwilling to venture any further. Drumming my fingers against the side of my hip, as I said, "So, I guess this is your . . . *palace*?" I scrunched up my nose and surveyed the place.

Taking in the thatched roof, the four dried-out bamboo sticks that supported it, the woven-grass mat that stood in as some sort of carpet, and the two brightly colored pillows he'd arranged in the center—surroundings so plain and humble, I have to admit that my already shaky faith in him took a pretty swift nosedive.

I mean, not to be rude or anything, but didn't he claim to be a *prince*?

Hadn't he actually made it a point to emphasize the word?

I watched as he busied himself in the corner, his back turned toward me as he took on some kind of task. Ignoring my comment, paying me absolutely no attention whatsoever, and it was then that I realized what I'd failed to see before.

Prince Kanta was crazy!

Like one of those poor, destitute, homeless people I sometimes saw wandering around and muttering to themselves back on the streets in the earth plane.

He was delusional.

Insane.

Living in some made-up fantasy world that existed only in his head—a world where princes dressed in rags and lived in shacks. Fully convinced he was some kind of royalty, when in fact, from what I could see, he was anything but. And apparently I'd been just dumb enough, just desperate enough for him to almost succeed in convincing me too.

I started to bolt, eager to get myself the heck out of there, when he turned, held his hands cupped before him, and offered me some kind of tea he'd just brewed.

I rose up on my tiptoes and peered at the dark, steaming liquid in the small yellow cup—saw the way the small bits of leaf clung to each other and collected around the edges. My eyes narrowing in suspicion as every warning I'd ever heard about the dangers of taking candy from strangers, especially completely wacko, psycho strangers, came back to haunt me. (Never mind the fact that my being dead ensured I could no longer be harmed in that way.)

"Take it." He thrust it upon me as he reached for a cup of his own. Lowering himself onto the blue patterned cushion in one quick, fluid move, he patted the orange one with the large starburst design just beside it. "Now sit," he commanded.

I knew better.

Knew I should take that opportunity to get myself the heck out of there. Take advantage of my proximity to the entry and just hit it while I could.

But instead, for some inexplicable reason, I found myself sitting right down beside him. Obediently crossing my legs as I held the warm cup in my hands.

He blew on the liquid, probably more out of habit and ritual than actual necessity, gazing out at those turquoise waters for what seemed like a very long time. Gazing at the sea for so long I was starting to get more than a little bit antsy. Starting to get more than a little annoyed with the whole situation. Sure that there was no way some dumb Mad-Hatter-style tea party could do anything toward helping me free my friends. If anything, it was the exact opposite—it was all amounting to a big waste of time.

And I was just about to express those feelings when he looked at me and said, "Drink." Probably figuring since I'd already gone along with his earlier commands, I'd just blindly go along with that too.

But I was done being bossed around. Done being treated like one of his royal subjects, and I was just about to start making a few demands of my own when he turned, looked me right in the eye, and said it again.

"*Drink.*"

I tried to break his gaze, but couldn't.

Tried to get to my feet and get myself out of there, but I couldn't do that either.

It was as though his eyes were holding me captive, paralyzed, in the strangest of ways. And the more I tried to fight it, the more I realized just how useless it was.

The word came at me again:

Drink.

His stare deepening as he plucked a loose thread from his robe and dropped it right into my cup.

And even though the sight of it disgusted me, even though I made my disgust known by shouting out, "*Ew!*"—even though not one single part of me actually consented to the act—my hands somehow magically lifted, rose from my lap to my mouth, where I tilted the cup, brought it to my parted lips, and allowed the liquid to seep out.

Drink.

The word swirling, repeating, clouding my head, my vision, my will—until the cup fell from my fingers, drained of its contents, and my body collapsed to the ground.

9

I was surrounded by mist. Thick, white, shimmering mist. My eyes squinting, straining, striving to see my way past it, vaguely aware of some place I needed to be just on the other side of it.

Some important destination he urged me to reach.

I pushed forward, my hands sweeping before me, trying to clear the space by batting away all the haze. My first few attempts yielded no success whatsoever, in fact, if anything, they just seemed to make the fog grow thicker, but then, little by little, it began to fade away until I found myself standing before a simple, but still rather impressive castle, like a fortress with a sturdy stone wall all around it.

"Is this it? Is this what you wanted me to see?" I glanced over my shoulder at Prince Kanta, seeing him nod in reply.

And there was something about the way he observed it, something about the way his eyes creased, the way his throat bobbed just a little—something about the way he held himself so silent and still—that told me that to him anyway, this was more than some random old palace we'd just stumbled upon.

His face wore an expression I knew all too well.

It was the same expression I sometimes wore when I snuck into the Viewing Room back in the Here & Now, where I hunkered down in one of those curtained off cubicles, sat on one of those hard metal stools, punched in my desired location, and watched the daily goings-on of my sister and friends back home on the earth plane.

It was the look of resolved longing.

The kind of look you get when you realize that the one thing you loved most in the world can never be yours.

"So, you really were a prince." I looked at him with a renewed sense of awe along with a good dose of guilt. Feeling terrible for still having not learned my lesson about judging by appearances and choosing to doubt him based purely on his clothes and the hut he chose to live in. But still, it's not like I could really be blamed for the verdict when all the evidence so clearly pointed against him.

"I was indeed." He nodded, turning his back to the scene. "I was indeed."

He waved at me, then started to lead us away, but after working so hard to get there, I wasn't quite ready to ditch it so soon.

"That's it?" My brow quirked as I tilted my head and threw my hands up by my sides. "You seriously went to all the trouble of drugging me with your special tea, only so you could give me a quick peek at some old castle, then try to convince me to leave? Because excuse me for saying so, but it seems like the least you could do after putting me through all of that is to give me a tour, show me around a bit. At least get me past the big gate, I mean— *sheesh*!"

I started to shake my head, started to roll my eyes, not quite completing the loop before he said, "There is plenty more to see, trust me on that." His large dark eyes bore down on mine. "But there is nothing more to see *here*. This place no longer exists. It's been gone for many centuries now. You must understand, Riley, that everything on the earth plane is impermanent. *Every. Thing.* The only thing you can ever count on in the physical world is *change*. Change is the only constant there is."

He raised his hand high and pointed to something just past my shoulder. And I turned to find the sky that just a moment ago had been hazy but clear, turned thick with smoke, while the place where the palace once stood was reduced to a pile of rubble and dust, as the ground just beneath ran red with blood.

"We were invaded," he told me, his voice steady and sure. And when I looked at him again, I noticed that the tattered old rags had returned, replacing the elegant tunic he'd manifested earlier. "As a result, I ended up here."

"On the island?" I scrunched up my nose, surprised to find myself suddenly returned to the beach once again. Only it was different. Different in a way I couldn't quite put my finger on.

He nodded, wordlessly pointing toward a very large house on a hill. A big, looming plantation-style home—like the kind you see in movies or in textbooks—which while not near as big as the palace he'd just shown me, still held a fair amount of square footage from what I could tell.

I glanced between Prince Kanta and the house, knowing it was supposed to mean something, symbolize something, but not quite sure what that was. "So, basically you went from an African palace, to a Caribbean plantation house, to the thatched roof hut on the beach, where, for whatever reason, you choose to live now." I turned, my eyes traveling the long, tall length of him, but he just remained silent and still. "I mean, you do *choose* to live there, right? Because if not, if you're really not all that happy with that kind of . . ." I paused, searching for just the right word that wouldn't come off as overly judgmental or offensive, but unable to come up with anything quick, I went on to say, "Anyway, you do know that you can manifest a whole new place just as easily as you can manifest the clothes you wear?" I looked at him, trying to read his face, but didn't get much of anything. "A stone, a castle, there's no limit—all you have to do is envision it, *see* yourself having it, and it's yours—easy-peasy!"

He turned away. Turned until his back was facing me. And I have to say, that really annoyed me since I wasn't quite done with my pitch. If anything, I was just getting started, was just about to inform him of my position as a Soul Catcher, and offer to escort him to the bridge as soon as this was all over.

But just as I was about to launch into all that, he glanced over his shoulder, pressed his finger to his lips, and pointed straight ahead as he whispered, "You make too much noise, Miss Riley Bloom. And because of it, you miss the whole point. Just watch. Don't speak. Allow the story to come to you."

Okay, in all honesty, that about quadrupled my annoyance. I mean, here he'd led me away from my friends who were in desperate need of my help, only to distract me with some freaky tea and a random collection of *not-so*-impressive pieces of real estate he was determined to show me.

And now he was telling me that I talk too much and to basically shut up?

Or at least that's how it sounded to me.

And yet, despite all that, for some reason I found my lips clamping together as my gaze followed the tip of his pointing finger all the way to where a man who looked *exactly* like Prince Kanta, a man who, after a few moments of observation, I realized *was* Prince Kanta, spent what must've been some major backbreaking days working the fields.

"I—I don't get it," I blurted, remembering too late how he didn't want me to speak. But still, I was confused and in need of some answers, and he was the only one around who was able to give them. "I thought you were a prince? I thought you lived in that castle in Africa?" He looked at me, nodding in confirmation. "So why would you leave a cushy life like that only to come here to get beaten and whipped no matter how hard you work?"

But then it hit me.

Before he could answer, the reason became clear.

Prince Kanta may have moved to this island, but it wasn't by choice.

Prince Kanta may have been a ruler in Africa, but in this place, he didn't even rule his own life.

He'd gone from a luxurious life of nobility—to the horrid life of a slave.

Forced to work the plantation from sunup to sunset and suffer terrible beatings whenever he was unfortunate enough to displease his master.

"Impermanence." He nodded, tearing his eyes away from the bleak scene in order to look into mine. "It's like I said earlier, nothing lasts forever, Riley. Where we begin is not always the same as where we end."

I gulped—an old habit left over from my time on the earth plane—as I turned away from the prince and watched the horrible scene that unfolded before me. Watched a series of beatings, inhumane acts of torture, including one that was so unspeakable, so barbaric, so unimaginably cruel, I was sure it couldn't be real. I was sure he was seriously pushing the truth just to make an impression on me.

But despite my best effort to look away, despite my turning my back, shutting my eyes, and placing my hands over my ears to drown out those awful, tormented, agonized cries—despite all of those avoidance techniques I employed—there was just no escaping it.

No matter how hard I tried to shield myself from it, the scene continued to play out before me—behind me—around me—inside me.

And since there was no way to stop it, no way to silence it, I was left with no choice but to allow it to run till its end.

So I watched.

Watched as a group of slaves were rounded up, ones

who'd been deemed disobedient, troublesome in a way that angered the plantation owner.

Watched as they were hauled over to a long, pristine expanse of beach where they were buried up to their necks in white sand.

Watched as a cruel and sadistic master, along with his friends, enjoyed a game of "bowling"—using the slaves' exposed heads as pins.

Watched as one slave after another succumbed to a tragically horrendous, untimely death.

It was hideous.

The true definition of *gruesome*.

And it was hard to imagine that anyone could enjoy something so cruel.

Yet, there it was, a revolting piece of history playing out before me. And thankfully, after a few moments of watching, Prince Kanta was kind enough to remove it from my view.

But even though I was no longer forced to watch, the images lingered, continuing to play in my head. Leaving me sickened, saddened, and so incredibly angry to think it went on for as long as it had, and that no one even once tried to stop it.

I was just about to express those very thoughts, just about to tell the prince how very sorry I was when a new scene appeared.

One in which the tables were turned.

One in which the oppressed rose up, gathered together, and systematically overcame their oppressors.

A revolt was in progress—the slaves versus the masters.

And if I'd still had a heart beating inside me, that would've been the moment when it lifted and skipped. Released of the weighty scene I'd watched only a moment earlier, I felt lighter, brighter, sure that I was about to see some much needed justice.

The first one to go was that sadistic plantation owner. And I'd be lying if I said I didn't raise my fist in the air and pump it with joy.

But it wasn't long before my joy turned to something else entirely, when Prince Kanta placed his hand over mine and slowly lowered it back to my side, silently nodding toward the scene that played next.

The one of the master's daughter—who went just after her dad.

A girl I figured to be around the same age as me.

A girl with curly brown hair, deep hazel eyes, a long, elegant nose, an overly embellished dress with a big yellow bow that slashed across the middle, and a small black dog by her side.

A girl I immediately recognized as Rebecca.

10

When I opened my eyes, I found myself positioned in a way that left me staring directly at Prince Kanta's calloused bare feet. My cheek pressed hard against the woven-grass mat, my body still toppled on its side.

And that's when I realized that despite all the things I'd just seen, I hadn't actually gone anywhere.

Hadn't stepped foot off the beach, or even out of his hut for that matter.

The tea was the journey.

I scrambled to get myself together, rearranging my limbs until I was upright again. Gazing at Prince Kanta, who sat right before me, as a mess of conflicting emotions ran amok in my head.

I was speechless.

Completely gobsmacked and speechless.

Which, if you've followed me to this point, then you know is not exactly a feeling I'm used to.

But to Prince Kanta's credit, it's not like he tried to rush me. In fact, he seemed pretty content to just remain right there on his pillow, legs crossed, feet propped up on his knees, as he calmly observed the ceaseless lull and sway of the sea. Allowing me all the time I could possibly need to make some kind of sense out of all the horrible things I'd just seen.

"So Rebecca haunts the earth plane because she was murdered?" I ventured, figuring I had to start somewhere and that was as good a place as any. "And if so, is that why you haunt it too?"

He faced me, observing me with that infinite gaze of his. Holding the look for so long that I started to grow a little antsy, a little uneasy, until he finally said, "Not exactly."

I scrunched my brow up under my bangs and waited for him to elaborate in some way. But when he didn't, when he just continued to sit there, I decided to press full speed ahead and say, "So, I guess I really don't get it then. I mean, why is she here? What's the point of the bubble and . . . and all the rest?" I winced at the way my voice cracked in the middle, knowing it revealed the full extent of my desperation to make some kind of sense of it.

Back on my very first assignment as a Soul Catcher, it didn't take long to learn how knowing a ghost's motivations, their reasons for lingering behind on the earth plane, could only help when it came time to dealing with them. And seeing how Rebecca had trapped my friends, well, I was more than a little eager to learn just what it was that motivated her.

So I waited. Waited for what felt like a ridiculously long stretch of the most agonizing silence. Waited until Prince Kanta finally looked at me and said, "Rebecca haunts the earth plane because she is angry. Very, *very* angry. And while it's true that her anger is a result of her murder, the murder itself is not what keeps her bound here. The anger alone is responsible for that."

Okay, on one level I got it, but on the other, I really didn't. And knowing he wasn't the type to just give away the answers, that he pretty much insisted I work for them, I said, "So, is that why you stay behind too? Because you're also angry about what happened to you?"

I clutched my hands in my lap, nervously entwining my fingers. Seeing the way his face transitioned through a variety of expressions, sure I'd somehow insulted him, overstepped some sort of unseen boundary, when he did pretty much the last thing I expected.

He smiled.

Okay, maybe it was more of a half smile.

But still, his cheeks widened, his lips lifted and curled at the sides, just enough to encourage those twin dimples to spring into view. It was all right there before me—the full on beginnings of what could've resulted in a truly lovely grin—but then he dropped that smile so quickly I was left wondering if it really had occurred.

"In the beginning, I was kept here by my anger, yes." He nodded, face solemn and serious once again. "But no longer."

I sat with his words, tossing them around in my head, going over them carefully, repeating them silently again and again. But despite all my efforts, despite my analyzing as best I could, I was still no closer to understanding just about anything he'd said.

Obviously, I got the part about anger being the glue that bound Rebecca here and that used to bind him here as well, and bippidy blah-blah. I mean, *duh,* it's not like I'm stupid. But what I didn't get was that if he was no longer angry, if he was no longer bound to the earth plane in that particular way, then why stay? Why hang on to such a horrifying past, when it was just as easy to move on to something else—something better than what he currently had?

Figuring I'd take one last stab at offering my services, I looked at him and said, "So, if you've moved past your anger, then why not cross the bridge already? I mean, I'm not trying to brag or anything, but getting people to the other side is pretty much my specialty."

I couldn't help but smile when I said it; I felt so empowered by the words. Reminded that I had a purpose, one that I was actually good at, and for a moment anyway, it lessened some of the guilt I had for getting my friends trapped.

But Prince Kanta would have none of it, and if he was impressed by my area of expertise, well, let's just say, he did a pretty good job of hiding it from me.

Apparently, he had no interest in the bridge, the Here & Now, or anything of the sort. He seemed perfectly content just making do with the funky grass hut, the shabby clothes, and the freaky tea.

"I cannot be free until my brothers and sisters are also free." The words simple, crisp, spoken in an accent that was really starting to grow on me. And yet I couldn't help but feel as though they weren't quite what they first seemed.

It was as though he was speaking in riddles.

As though he was hiding something from me.

And that's pretty much all it took to ignite my suspicions again.

"Too many remain stuck here. I cannot enjoy my release until they are also released," he added, though the words didn't do much to appease me.

It's like, if he was so reluctant to move on, then fine, whatever, his choice. I mean, maybe Bodhi was right—maybe I should just stick with the jobs the Council assigned, and ignore all the other lingering souls I happened to come across.

All I knew for sure was that for every minute I spent in that hut talking nonsense with the prince and viewing scenes that had nothing to do with me, I lost another sixty seconds during which I could've been helping my friends.

I rose to my feet, my voice agitated, a little bit *angry* even, when I stared right at Prince Kanta and said, "Listen, excuse me for saying so, but I don't really get why you couldn't have just told me all that from the start. I mean, why all this?" I waved my arm before me. "Why drag me out here to drink your freaky tea, when you could've just summarized the whole thing back in the graveyard?" I glared, knowing my emotions were starting to get the best of me, but at that moment, I didn't really care. "I mean, it's not like you don't know that my friends are trapped and in desperate need of my help, and yet, instead of offering the help that you promised, you choose to drag me out here just so you could totally waste my time." I shook my head and made for the doorway, not even bothering to look over my shoulder when I said, "Listen, if you ever feel like leaving this place, let me know. I'll see if there's room in my schedule."

I had every intention of bolting, had placed one foot firmly outside of that hut, but I was soon stopped by his voice when he said, "The tea is called *memory tea*."

I paused, glancing over my shoulder to find him shooting me a pointed look.

"And you are right, I could have just told you the story. That would have been easy enough. But I chose the tea for a reason. I wanted you to observe the story on your own, rather than to hear my possibly biased version. I also could have immersed you in the scene and let you experience it directly, but I thought it too horrific, too frightening for a child your age. Besides, that sort of thing is more Rebecca's domain."

I narrowed my eyes into slits. Narrowed my eyes till I could just barely make out the tall, dark outline of him. And even though I'm sure his words made all the sense in the world to his ears—to mine, not so much.

It was just another riddle.

More craftily worded nonsense that made me doubt him even more.

I folded my arms across my chest, screwed my lips to the side, and took another step forward. Stopped again by the sound of his voice when he said, "Words have the power to harm or heal, Riley. They can be used to paint many emotional landscapes. And they are often influenced, if not biased, by the speaker. It was necessary for you to experience the story with your own eyes, to view it through your own filter, your own set of biases and prejudices, and to not be influenced by mine. There is nothing like being a true witness to something to gain your own unique understanding of it. So tell me, Riley, were you not moved by what you saw? I'm curious to hear your perception of it."

I was more than ready to bolt, eager to get back to that snow globe from hell where Bodhi and Buttercup were in desperate need of my help. But just like before, the one thing I wanted most at that moment happened to be in direct opposition to the one thing I did.

Instead of leaving, instead of bidding adios to the prince, I turned, turned until I was looking right at him again, and tried to explain the confusing array of emotions I'd felt—emotions I would happily choose never to experience again. But now that I'd felt them, now that those awful scenes had entered my mind, I knew there was no getting rid of them.

Later, they might get tucked away somewhere dark and not often visited, but it's not like they'd ever really vanish completely. It's not like they'd ever disappear.

Once introduced, they'd stay with me forever.

There was no emotional dumping ground for that sort of thing.

And before I knew it, I was back in the hut. Leaning against one of the bamboo sticks that held up the roof, avoiding his gaze as I searched for a way to explain. Part of me wanting to say something sassy, snarky—the kind of thing my mom refers to as *mouthy*.

I mean, how did he think I perceived what I'd seen? How would any sane person—either living or dead—perceive it?

The words practically leapt off my tongue, begging to be heard, but then, when I looked at him again, when my blue eyes stared into his dark brown ones, well, those words disappeared as a whole string of new ones jumped into their place.

"At first, I was amazed that you were really a prince. I thought for sure you lied about that." I snuck a quick peek at him, relieved to see that he looked a lot closer to amused than offended, which I took as a sign to continue. "I felt awful when you lost everything, and even worse when I saw the beatings you suffered. And when the revolt began, well, I was seriously ready to cheer, but then . . ." I hesitated, seeing the way he urged me on with his rising brow and nodding head. "But then, it all started to seem like some horrible cycle of violence. Especially when I realized that the slaves were revolting so they could take over and bring in a whole new set of slaves. And it just seemed so pointless. Like a battle no one could ever truly win. An endless cycle of abuse, and it left me really sad."

He half smiled again. Reminding me of the way the sun would peek out from the clouds on an overcast day on the earth plane, just long enough to bestow a brief hint of warmth before disappearing again and turning everything gray.

And that's pretty much the exact moment when my second goal was added.

After making sure that Bodhi and Buttercup were freed from Rebecca's trap, I was determined to see the prince smile for reals.

Watching as he rose quickly to his feet and said, "You are right. It is a vicious cycle indeed. During my reign as prince, I kept my own set of slaves until my castle was invaded and I was sold as a slave and sent here—only to revolt against my master with the hope of taking over the island and enslaving others in the same way I'd been." He shook his head and took his time in looking me over. "I have seen both sides of this madness, and now, after sharing that with you, and because of your deep understanding, you are ready to make the journey inside Rebecca's world."

II

"You will never succeed with such a method. You are going about it all wrong."

We were standing just outside of the bubble—

No, scratch that.

The truth is Prince Kanta was standing just outside the bubble while *I* was pressed up against it, pounding and kicking the smooth, glossy exterior with every bit of my (undeniably measly) strength.

I glanced over my shoulder, not even trying to hide my annoyance. "Oh, yeah? So why don't you come over and help instead of just standing there watching me fail. Why don't you show me how it's done, if you know so much?"

But the prince made no move to help. He just remained right where he was. Neither flinching nor wincing—not reacting to my tone or my words in any way, shape, or form. In fact, he was so still and serious, I actually wondered if he'd heard me. Though I'd yelled it so loudly, I was pretty sure it'd been impossible to miss.

I'd just turned back to the globe and was about to start pounding again when he said, "You will never succeed with resistance, Riley. In this case, as in most cases, resistance just begets more resistance. Or, in other words, what you resist—persists. Acceptance is the only way."

Oh, brother.

I rolled my eyes and shook my head, annoyed to the point where I no longer cared if he saw.

As far as I was concerned, it was just a whole lot of psychobabble, more crazy talk *coming right up*, and it was getting me nowhere. For whatever reason, rather than actually helping me, he'd chosen to distract me, annoy me, and just generally waste my time. And once again, I'd found that I'd pretty much reached my limit with him.

I narrowed my gaze, glaring at him in such a way that I wouldn't have been the least bit surprised if great plumes of smoke shot out from my nose and my ears. My voice harsh, edgy, making absolutely no further attempt at good manners, little niceties, or the smallest of pleasantries, when I said, "Listen, maybe you mean well, maybe you don't, only you know for sure. But either way, I think you need to know that I'm pretty much done listening to these crazy philosophical riddles that I doubt even you understand." I pushed my long, side-swept bangs off my face, tried to tuck them back behind my ears, but being just a smidgen too short, they fell right back into my eyes, so I decided to leave them there. "So either you help me break into this bubble so I can free my friends, or—"

Our eyes met.

"Or you . . . *don't*." I lifted my shoulders, knowing that as far as threats went, it was a pretty pathetic one, but still, at that moment, it was the best I could do. "Either way, I have no time to waste, so if you don't mind—"

I returned to the bubble, my fist rising high above my head, just about to bring it back down and smash it hard against the side, when it was caught in midair by the prince.

His fingers circled my wrist, as his eyes bore into mine. Then slowly, with no cooperation on my part, he unfolded my fingers, one at a time. Straightening and spreading them as he lowered my palm and gently placed it onto the bubble until it was flush against the surface, his face calm, eyes kind, softly cooing in a way that strangely sent a soothing wave of calm coursing through me.

"*Shhh . . .*" He looked at me. "You must remain quiet, peaceful, and still. You must accept the situation you now find yourself in. All of this fighting—all of this *resistance*—is only making it worse. Rebecca thrives on anger. It is the fuel that fires her world. And you, Miss Riley Bloom, are only aiding her." He paused for a moment, long enough to make sure I was listening, before he continued. "Your friends are trapped, there is no getting around that. But rather than fighting what *is*, you must first learn to accept it. Only then will you clear a path in your mind that will lead you to the solution."

I looked at him, looked right into those deep, mysterious eyes, and I started to say: *What?*

Started to say: *Are you crazy? Why should I even think about accepting such a horrible thing—when I have to do whatever it takes to stop it?*

But before I could get to any of that, the strangest thing happened.

The bubble's surface, the reflective, rounded part that lay just under my fingers, began to soften and give just the tiniest bit.

I looked at Prince Kanta, my eyes wide, jaw practically dropped to my knees, seeing him nod, press his finger briefly to his lips, and then motion for me to place my other hand just beside it.

So I did.

And the same thing happened again.

The surface continuing to soften and give as he said, "Rather than fighting the bubble, you must learn to accept it." He moved into place, positioning himself right next to me, and pressing his palms against it in the same way I did. "Are you familiar with the cornstarch-and-water experiment?"

I looked at him, my voice high-pitched and screechy as I blurted, "Oobleck!" Remembering the day at summer camp when the counselors separated us all into small groups, then handed us each a bowl filled with a pile of cornstarch and water they'd mixed together, and how surprised I was when they told us to make a fist and pound on it as hard as we could, only to find my fist bouncing right back. It was impossible to penetrate, or at least not by force anyway. "If you try to force your way into the mix by pounding it or jabbing it, it doesn't work. It . . . *resists*." My eyes grew wide as I gazed at him, suddenly understanding what he'd been trying to tell me all along. "But if you press slowly and gently—"

"Then your fingers sink right in." He nodded, his expression showing how pleased he was that I finally understood, even though he refused to grant me a smile. "So you must think of the bubble as this—"

"Oobleck." I nodded.

"You must *accept* that your friends are inside, *accept* that Rebecca is very angry and will do all that she can to work against you, *accept* all of that as your current reality, and then once you've accepted what *is*, you are free to proceed without the need to force anything." He paused, making sure I understood, and I'm happy to say that I did.

"There are many trapped inside, many others whom you've never met, but who are in need of your help nonetheless. I must tell you that I have dreamed that the glowing ones would arrive one day, and now that you are here, I am very much pleased."

He continued to speak, but I was no longer listening. All I could focus on was the part about the *glowing ones*.

While my glow may not have been *all that*—while it may have only been a *barely there* green (as Bodhi was so quick to point out)—it was there nonetheless.

Radiant enough to where even Prince Kanta had seen it.

Radiant enough to where he thought I might be of some help.

"Once we are inside, in order to help them, in order to *release* them, we must learn the stories that keep them imprisoned in order to compassionately free them from their own pasts."

I looked at him, acknowledging that while he was definitely weird, a bit of an oddball for sure, I was still glad to have him around, since I was pretty sure that, glow or no glow, I wasn't really all that equipped to tackle the job on my own.

I watched as he pressed up against the bubble, moved

himself so close his entire body, including his nose and his face, were pressed flush against it. Then, with a quick wave of his fingers, he motioned for me to follow suit.

And after positioning myself the same way as he had, we closed our eyes and melded with the surface, and not long after, we found ourselves inside.

12

It was different from before.

Last time it'd been more personal.

An exact replica of my kindergarten classroom.

A hell made exclusively for me.

And though the scenery had suffered some pretty dramatic changes, I was relieved to find it changed in a more general, less individual kind of way.

While it wasn't exactly the hell of flames and pitchforks and devils' horns one might expect when visiting such a place, it was still dark and dreary and hellish in its own right.

It was also so quiet and desolate and calm, I had the odd sensation of being plopped down in the middle of a still life or landscape. Only instead of the glistening streams and sun-dappled gardens you often see in oil paintings, this one was a completely dry and barren scene. Created from a palette of varying shades of blacks, grays, and deep reddish browns—like a forest unable to overcome the lasting effects of a fire that raged a long time before. Leaving nothing but burned-out tree carcasses, dried up lake beds, and a never-ending deluge of thick squares of ash that rose and swirled and circled and swooped only to fall once again.

"Where are we?" I whispered. Even though I didn't see Rebecca or anyone else, for some reason, I was afraid of being overheard.

"We are inside her world." Prince Kanta turned till he was facing me, his mouth drawn, face serious, as he said, "Both Rebecca's heart and soul have become so soiled with anger and hate, this is the result."

I looked all around, curious to see what else there might be, how far it might go, and if it was actually possible to see the rounded, sloping smooth walls that separated us from everything else. But while I couldn't see much of anything besides a whole lot of scorched earth, it's not like I was curious enough to venture off on my own. I was far too reluctant to leave the prince's side, and though I had no way of knowing just how bad it might get, I was pretty sure this was only the beginning of what that evil, little ghost girl had in store.

Besides, it's not like I had time for a tour. I needed to find Bodhi and Buttercup as quickly as possible, so we could get the heck out of there.

"Does she know we're here?" I asked, sensing the answer well before I saw his nodding head.

"Oh, yes. This is her world. She is aware of everything that occurs here."

"So what now?" I gazed up at the prince and bit down on my lip, hoping he'd have a good idea or two, since I hadn't a clue. "Where do we find them? Where do we go? What do we do?"

But even though I was fully resolved to following his lead, Prince Kanta just looked at me and said, "The journey is mostly here." He tapped the side of his head, the space between his temple and ear, before adding, "And less here." He arced his arm out before him, motioning toward an expanse of scorched earth.

And seeing that, well, I have to admit it took pretty much all of my willpower not to groan and roll my eyes, but somehow I refrained. No matter how grateful I was to have him around, there was no doubt he was a bit of a nutcase. Still, he had been through an awful lot, experienced the kind of things that would definitely end up testing the sanity of just about anybody, and so, with that in mind, I decided to do my best not to judge, which, I hate to admit, was really quite a stretch for me.

So instead I just said, "Um, care to translate?"

Watching as he moved until he was standing a few feet before me, taking a moment to survey the land with his hand pressed tightly against his brow, shielding his eyes from the deluge of ash that continued to fall. Then dropping his hand just as quickly, he snatched up an old, burned-out tree branch from the ground, using the pointy broken end to draw a small circle deep into a bed of ash as he said, "This circle represents you." He glanced at me, making sure I understood, before he went on to draw a much bigger circle just outside of it. "And this is the bubble."

I nodded. So far, so good, I was able to follow.

Then after drawing a zigzaggy line that filled up the entire area between the small and large circles he added, "And somewhere in here are your friends."

"Yeah, Bodhi and Buttercup," I said, eager to get on with it, sure he was just about to get to the good part—the part that would tell me exactly where to find them.

"And so, knowing what you know about this Bodhi and . . . *Buttercup.*" My dog's name sounding almost hilariously foreign on his tongue, he tapped the ground with his stick and asked, "Where would you begin looking for them? What would be the very last place they'd ever want to revisit? What would be the place that holds the most trauma—the most anger for them?"

My cheeks began to flush, and I quickly averted my gaze.

I had no idea how to answer, and I couldn't help but feel deeply embarrassed for that.

Sure, Bodhi's untimely death by bone cancer seemed like the obvious choice, but when I remembered the casual way in which he told me, the way he just shrugged it off and said something like, "But that's the way it goes sometimes, right?" well, I wasn't so sure.

I mean, was that just a bit of bravado?

Some big, phony, tough-guy act he put on because he wanted me to respect him and make a good impression?

Had he really been so accepting of his early demise?

Or did that acceptance come only after the point when he could no longer change it—when he was already dead and couldn't do a dang thing about it?

Because when it came down to my own untimely exit, I fully admit that even though I was learning my place and finding my way on the other side, I still had my moments when I couldn't help but feel outraged that I'd never, ever get to be the only thing I really wanted to be: *thirteen*.

The only real, actually feasible, seemingly attainable goal that I'd had was to be a bonafide, real-deal teenager—and just like *that* it was stolen from me.

But still, maybe that was just me. As far as I knew, Bodhi had an entirely different way of seeing these things.

I turned back to Prince Kanta, my shoulders lifting as

I said, "There was a girl. A really pretty, dark-haired girl. And even though I knew it was Rebecca in disguise, Bodhi couldn't see that. To him, it was someone he recognized, and he raced after her like . . ." I paused long enough to re-play the scene in my head, remembering the look on his face, the longing in his voice, before I looked back at the prince and said, "He raced after her like he really, really missed her. Though I'm afraid I don't know anything more."

The prince's gaze narrowed and darted as though he was alerted to a sudden change in the area, his back stiffening, shoulders squaring, as he said, "Now just keep that in mind. No matter what happens next, no matter where you find yourself, just stay focused on your friend. Do *not* allow her to get to you. Do *not* allow her to introduce anything personal. The moment you focus on yourself, the moment you let your mind stray from your friends, *you lose.*" He looked at me, our eyes meeting briefly before he looked away again. "Can you do that?" he asked.

And even though I wanted to smile and nod and give him two big thumbs-up along with a superconfident reply of *Heck yeah, I can do it, no problem—no problem at all!*

The reality is, I just stood there and gaped.

The words "The moment you let your mind stray from your friends, *you lose*"—running amok in my head.

Because the truth was, there was no denying the fact

that I wasn't all that great at staying focused. In fact, I had a really bad habit of jumping from one thing to the next. And as far as my thoughts were concerned, well, most of the time my mind was nothing but a big ol', jumbled-up mess.

But unfortunately, I didn't get to express those concerns. Instead, I just stood there, wide-eyed and mute, as Prince Kanta whispered, "She's here."

And that's the last thing I heard before I was separated from the prince and sucked even deeper into her world.

13

It's like, one moment I was standing before the prince like the world's biggest shell-shocked doofus, and the next I was somewhere entirely different. Noticing how the scorched landscape had made way for a carpet of patchy weeds and rich, red-tinged soil, while the relentlessly falling ash had transformed into a clear and sunny day, allowing me a beautiful view of a pristine blue lake.

I narrowed my eyes and gazed all around, seeing the still navy waters, the towering pine trees, the smoldering campfire . . . the memory of something nudging me, prodding me, as I gazed down at my clothing and took a quick inventory of faded hand-me-down jeans, mud-covered pink-and-silver sneakers, and a lime green sweatshirt with the sleeves yanked down well past the tips of my fingers in order to hide the charm bracelet I'd *borrowed* from my sister.

And suddenly, I need look no further.

I knew exactly where I was.

My last trip to the lake.

My last trip with my family.

The last place I ever visited—or at least as a living, breathing resident of the earth plane.

The last time I'd ever hugged my parents, played fetch with my dog, or joked around with my sister as a real, live, flesh-and-blood person.

The last time I'd ever be dumb enough to believe that the thing I'd looked forward to most—my thirteenth birthday— was just around the corner.

Everything about that scene feeling as real as it did that day.

Only it wasn't real. Not even close.

And while part of me knew that, it was only a very small part of me.

Somewhere inside, on some deep-down level, I knew I needed to turn away and focus on something else. Something extremely important. Something in need of my utmost attention.

But the truth was, I was so caught up in the scene, I could no longer remember what that important thing was.

Couldn't imagine anything more significant than focusing on the splendor that played out before me:

Buttercup running in circles and barking like crazy

before jumping into my dad's SUV and settling onto my knee.

Ever and I bickering and fighting and basically driving both our parents crazy.

Ever discovering she'd left her prized sky blue Pinecone Lake Cheerleading Camp sweatshirt behind, and begging my dad to turn the car around and head back to the lake so that she could retrieve it.

My dad agreeing to do just that despite his concerns about the traffic.

Me singing along to a Kelly Clarkson song I blasted on my iPod—partly because I liked it, and partly because it annoyed Ever.

A deer appearing out of nowhere, dashing right into our lane, as my father swerved to avoid it, smashed through the guardrail, down the embankment, and into a tree that left us all dead.

Me not realizing I was dead.

Me feeling so fine, and good, and alive that halfway across the bridge to the other side I changed my mind and went back to search through those vast fragrant fields for my sister.

Only to find she'd returned to the earth plane—to her body—to life.

Only to discover the horrifying truth that I no longer could.

A fact that made me so *angry,* the next thing I knew I was stuck in a moment of flaming red rage I was forced to relive over and over again.

A rage so deep, which burned so bright, it turned the once vibrating, pulsating field back into its original state of scorched, burned, and unforgivingly seared earth.

Prince Kanta's warning *The moment you let your mind stray from your friends, you lose* reduced to a long-forgotten memory.

Prince Kanta was gone.

He had no role in this story.

My entire world had been reduced to a small plot of land consisting of nothing more than my deep seething anger and me.

14

I sank to my knees, threw myself onto a large pile of ash that instantly blackened my clothes, and cried and screamed and cursed and wailed, just like I had then.

Though it's not like it brought my family back.

It's not like it returned me to the way I had been.

Still, I was unable to stop, unable to remove myself from the scene.

Unable to focus on anything other than the never-ending cycle of anger and rage that threatened to consume me.

If you asked how long it went on, well, the truth is, I have no idea. Somewhere between an eternity and a handful of seconds would be my best guess. Either way, it was far too long for me to be carrying on like I'd been.

But then, eventually, somewhere in the midst of all the shouting and tantrum throwing came a sort of break.

A brief respite that lasted a split second at best.

A brief respite that contained what I can only describe as a small patch of—*silence*.

A small, bright space where anger could not exist.

And though it only lasted a moment, from that moment on, a part of me was focused solely on waiting for it to happen again.

And when it did, it seemed to linger just a little bit longer.

And the time after that—longer still.

Until finally, that bright and tiny gap of *silence* stretched and grew until it expanded into a space just large enough for me to crawl into.

My rage stilled, and soon my anger disappeared, as everything around me and inside me began to settle and calm. Allowing me to observe my situation with such clarity, there was no denying the fact that I was not at all different from anyone else who got stuck in this place.

We were all just as angry and unforgiving as Rebecca wanted us to be.

I was connected to all of these lost and lonely souls just as sure as they were connected to me.

For that brief split second, I could see the truth of *everything*—and that's all it took to break free.

That's all it took to know that I wasn't alone, and never had been. I had nothing to fear, nothing to be angry about, and while it was true that I'd never expected my life to end up quite like it did, there was no denying the fact that in a lot of ways it'd ended up a lot better than I ever could've imagined.

I rose from my place, watching in astonishment as the scorched field gave way, revealing the bubble in its real and true state—so different from the view Rebecca wanted me to see.

No longer was there falling ash or burned-out trees that morphed into kindergarten classrooms, no longer were there vast and lonely fields, and family trips ending abruptly: There was nothing but a dark and murky crowded sea of wretched, writhing souls, each one trapped in a tormented hell of his or her own.

I moved among them, wondering what happened to the prince as I searched for Bodhi and Buttercup—eager to try and release them in the same way I'd been. Pushing through a throng of never-ending cycles of pain and misery and centuries-old suffering, as I struggled to hold my focus on what I'd just learned, what I needed to remember most, while suppressing my own rising panic that fought to summon my own darker impulses.

Then, just as quickly, I stopped. Stopped right in the middle of all that continuous pain and chaos, thinking that if it was true that we were all connected, then I shouldn't have to wander very far, if at all. I should be able to stay right where I was, keeping just calm enough and just quiet enough to tune in to this bubble of lost souls and, like the prince said, allow their stories to come forth.

So I shut my eyes tightly and tried to sort through the haze of frenetic energy in order to locate my dog and my guide.

And while I'm happy to report that it didn't take all that long to find Bodhi—being able to reach him was a whole 'nother matter.

15

I hung back, not quite sure how to proceed. Carefully observing Bodhi, who remained completely unaware of me.

His brow creased, his hands clenched into fists he held tightly to his sides, his lips quivering, teeth gnashing so hard together it rendered his long string of words impossible to decipher.

Knowing he probably wouldn't like it, knowing that as soon as he was released from whatever torment played out in his head, he'd find some lame excuse to rail on me about invading his privacy (or some other infraction, either real or imagined), I went in anyway.

Slowly inching my way toward him until I was close enough to reach for his balled-up hand and grasp it in mine, allowing my energy to stream and merge with his, until I'd eased my way inside his head.

At first, it was impossible to make sense of much of

anything. It was messy, chaotic, and extremely confusing—
like a super-disorganized bedroom with big piles of papers
and clothes and books and *stuff* littered all over the floor—
and it was a while before I was able to get myself settled and
get it all sorted out.

Unlike my thoughts (and my room!), which had always
been more or less orderly and clear, his weren't even close.
So, I went deeper, eventually sinking so far inside, it was as
though I'd become him.

I stood there, feeling tall and awkward as I tried to get
used to being inside his body, watching everything play
out before me as though it were actually happening to me.
Though it all seemed so random and confusing all I could
really make out was a school.

From the looks of the lockers and the hand-painted
signs that lined up and down the hallway where I stood—
all of them touting football games, bake sales, and upcoming
dances—I figured it was a high school.

Then, just after I'd finally nailed that, I was on the
move. Running with a pair of legs that were far more
powerful than the short, skinny ones I was used to, racing
to keep up with some girl whose long dark hair lifted and
waved in such a way, I'd convinced myself it was an
invitation to follow.

She slipped around a corner and into a library, and I

ducked in right behind her. Shielding myself behind the tall shelves of books, where I watched, part of me hoping she'd notice me, part of me hoping she wouldn't, willing to give just about anything to see what she scribbled so furiously into her notebook.

My eyes roamed her, noting the way her hair spilled over her shoulders, the way her backpack leaned against the leg of her chair, the way her boots were crusted with a thin layer of mud, the way her purple ballpoint pen continued to fly across a sheet of lined paper, as my mind swirled with words, declarations, things I longed to tell her but knew I never would.

Too scared to approach her, I chose to just watch her instead. My head spinning with a series of jumbled-up images, a long string of snapshots and phrases, trying to sort through all the random pieces of Bodhi's memory, the haphazard scrapbook of his brain.

I knew the girl was Nicole—the same girl whose image lured him into the bubble—but what I didn't know was what he could possibly be so angry about. I mean, in order to be trapped in Rebecca's world, you had to get pretty riled up about something. And, up to that point anyway, I hadn't seen a single thing worthy of that kind of rage.

I mean, was it the way she ignored him?

The way she pretended not to notice him, despite the fact that he made a point to always be where she was?

And if so, was that really worth getting all tripped up over?

While I obviously can't speak for Bodhi, I can say that for me, it all seemed a little ridiculous. And not being the most patient person in the world (not even close), well, the truth is, I started to get more than a little frustrated with him.

So frustrated I'd just made up my mind to pop right back out of his body and try to find another way to reach him, when his whole world went so dark and dim, I had to squint my eyes and strain my ears to make any kind of sense of it.

And still, even then, there were only four things I could really make out:

1. A bell
2. A girl
3. A boy
4. A body

Those four images repeating themselves like a series of fast takes caught in a continuous loop. Though no matter how many times I watched, none of it made any more sense than it had the first time around.

A bell—a girl—a boy—a body—

A quick snippet of each flashing over and over again.

And just when I couldn't take another second, couldn't bear another glimpse of it, the images became clearer, more defined, until they eventually settled into some kind of order—though it's not like it made it any easier.

I listened as the *bell* rang so loudly I actually winced at the sound of it.

I watched as a classroom door flew open and a *girl* I recognized as Nicole spilled out. Her shoulders stooped, head bent in a way that encouraged her long dark hair to provide cover for her tear-stained cheeks—the result of the long string of insults being hurled her way.

And while I wasn't the least bit surprised when I caught a glimpse of myself in a classroom window and realized that I—er, I mean, Bodhi—was the *boy* (I mean, after all, it was his memory I was experiencing), still, it was a version of Bodhi I wasn't quite used to seeing.

Though his outside appearance remained more or less the same—(maybe a little more solid, a little less filmy than how he usually looked)—it was still really odd to view him as a living, breathing person who could neither fly nor glow and had no idea that he someday would.

Never mind the fact that he was so incredibly unsure and insecure and overly preoccupied with coming off as cool—it was kind of hard to watch him (and even harder to *be* him) without feeling more than a little embarrassed for him.

But it was only a moment before the focus returned to Nicole.

Still crying.

Still stalked.

Still harassed by a group of classmates who followed her wherever she went.

Bullying her in a way that wasn't just a pattern of behavior—but a favorite pastime of theirs.

I stood off to the side, my voice rising above all the others as I heatedly defended her. Screaming at them to stop, to leave her alone, to find a better, more productive way to spend their free time. A better way to build themselves up.

And then the *bell* again . . .

The series of scenes continuing to repeat, and yet still not making the slightest bit of sense no matter how many times I watched them play.

Then, I remembered.

There was more.

A fourth scene I'd glimpsed only the haziest hint of . . .

A body.

And the next thing I knew, I was propelled from the school to a nice, modest house where a parade of cops and paramedics and crying, distraught people streamed in and out.

All of them hovering around a stretcher—like the kind you see in movies.

A stretcher holding a small, slim, sheet-covered, completely lifeless form . . .

And I knew without being told that the body was Nicole's, and that Bodhi blamed himself.

I fought my way out. So uncomfortable with being inside his guilt-ridden mind and self-hating skin, I was desperate to look him in the eyes and confront him myself.

Tugging hard on his arm as I said, "But you *tried*. You tried to stop it. I *saw* you—I *heard* you—I *was* you!" Practically screaming at him, so desperate to free him so that I too could be released from all this.

But Bodhi wasn't having it. He just shook his head, eyes blazing with anger, voice laced with bitterness, when he said, "Oh, really? And just exactly what is it you heard, Riley? What is it you *actually* said when you were me?"

I squinted, having no idea what he was getting at—I mean, hadn't we experienced the same thing?

Following the length of his pointing finger all the way to the place where it played out again.

A bell, a boy, a girl . . .

Finally realizing the truth:

The real reason no one reacted when Bodhi and I both screamed those words—the real reason we were so easily ignored.

We hadn't actually spoken them.

Hadn't uttered anything at all.

Those words never found their way out of Bodhi's mouth, much less past his heart.

I didn't know what to say. Didn't know how to even begin to try to comfort him.

All I knew for sure is that anger and guilt mixed together made for a pretty strong brew—one that could trap a person forever.

"I was gonna say something that day, I had it all planned out, but then, at the very last moment, I chickened out and put it off until Monday instead." His voice was solemn as he continued to stare straight ahead. "Figured I'd take the weekend to get up the courage to try and convince her that she was smart and beautiful and unique and cool, and that nothing those other kids said was the slightest bit true. I mean, don't get me wrong, I knew she didn't like me. Or at least, not in the way I liked her. I was just some stupid, runty freshman, and she was the exotic, older new girl." He swiped his palm across his face, across his eyes, and I quickly looked away, pretended not to notice. I just waited patiently beside him, sensing he might need a moment or two before he was ready to continue.

"I just wanted her to know I was on her side—but, as it turns out, I never got to say any of that because Monday never came. Or at least not for her, anyway."

I stood there beside him, watching a family entrenched in a grief so big and raw, it threatened to consume me as well.

"I guess she couldn't take it anymore, felt she had nowhere to turn. And so . . ." He looked at me, eyes filled with sadness as the words reverberated between us. "I went to her funeral." His shoulders slumped. "And I used to leave a flower in her mailbox every day on my way home from school, or at least until they moved, anyway."

"And those other kids? The bullies?" I asked, feeling almost as awful as he did.

He looked at me, shaking his head in a world-weary way. "Things were different back then. A slap on the wrist, an anti-bullying seminar in the school auditorium, and a whole lot of nonsense about how kids will be kids."

"And that's why you're stuck, then?" I scrunched up my nose and peered at him. "Because you think you were accountable?"

"I participated with my silence." He shrugged. "I *was* accountable. I did nothing to stop it."

To be honest, I had no idea what to do at that point—had no idea what to say. So, I did the only thing I could think of, I squeezed his hand tighter and imagined a small golden bubble of love and forgiveness shimmering all around him, remembering how it'd worked once before, and hoping it would work once again.

And when he looked at me, well, that's when I saw it. Saw the hate and anger being edged out by the small glimmer of *silence* displayed in his gaze.

"Hold on to it," I urged. "Hold on to the silence for as long as you can. There's no room for the bad stuff in there."

And the next thing I knew, he was back. Answering the thought in my head about whether he'd ever seen her again, when he said, "The Here & Now is a big place, Riley." He looked away, running his hand through his hair, before plucking that chewed-up green straw from his shirt pocket and popping it between his front teeth. "I thought I saw her once from a distance, but that's it."

I squinted, wanting more. Unable to believe he'd just leave it like that.

"I didn't approach her if that's what you're getting at. And I really don't think I should have to explain myself."

"But why not?" I gazed up at him, surprised to still find the smallest trace of the insecure boy he had been, or at least where Nicole was concerned. "Why not talk to her? You'd think she'd be glad to see you—a familiar face if nothing else."

"Trust me, there's nothing familiar about me. She didn't even know I existed." He bit down hard on the straw, clearly frustrated with me. "It's high-school stuff, Riley. Stuff you wouldn't understand."

I rolled my eyes and turned away, but not without letting him see just how angry that made me. Honestly, that was a pretty low blow. I mean, it's not like it was my fault I'd never be thirteen, in fact, it's not like—

I scowled at the ground, my anger rising, flaring, threatening to consume me completely, and that's when I noticed a patch of scorched earth beginning to spread just under my feet. And that's when I stopped those thoughts right in their tracks, watching in astonishment when the scorched earth disappeared once again.

Focus, vigilance, concentration—just like the prince said.

I had to guard against my temper, my anger, and Bodhi did too. This place encouraged it, thrived on it, whether it was justified or not, it didn't make a difference. As far as Rebecca was concerned, it was fuel all the same.

"Can you see it?" I asked, not sure which world he was in: the one of old high schools, scorched earth, or the one I could see—the one of lost and tormented souls.

He nodded, looking all around, seeing there were hundreds of them, then sighing as he said, "We need to find Buttercup and get the heck out of here."

But I quickly shook my head. While I may not understand the world of tragic high-school romance, thanks to Prince Kanta this horrible world of hate I did understand.

"No." I looked at Bodhi. "First we need to find Butter-cup, then we need to find my friend the prince, then we need to find a way to free all of them." I motioned toward the sea of tormented souls as Bodhi stood beside me and winced, adding, "And only after we've done all of that, can we even think about leaving this place."

16

Having known him since he was just a tiny pup, I gotta say, I had a pretty hard time believing that Buttercup could have anything to be angry about.

Even compared to all the other well-cared for pets on our block, there was no doubt he'd lived the cushiest, most insanely pampered life of them all. One that had no shortage of doggy treats, car rides with the windows rolled down, and nice outdoor spots for napping in the sun. And the times we did play pranks on him—like the times Ever and I dressed him up for the holidays in Santa, Easter Bunny, or even Cupid costumes, or the time we dabbed a chunk of peanut butter onto the tip of his nose and laughed ourselves silly as we watched him bark and run circles as he struggled to lick it off—well, you could tell he was in on the joke.

You could tell he was having fun.

So why we found him all curled up into a tight little ball of angst, with his eyes shut tight, teeth gnashing together, paws trashing and kicking as he whined and whimpered like he was the object of the most horrifying torture was beyond me.

Buttercup had never been tortured. Never been given a reason to carry on like that. And, to be honest, it kind of annoyed me to see him acting like he had.

But when I saw the way the trees started to appear again, the whole burned-out, shriveled-up sight of them, I tossed that feeling aside and instead dropped down to my knees.

I was staring at my dog, having no idea what to do, when Bodhi said, "What's his problem?" He glanced between Buttercup and me with a confused expression that served as a perfect match for my own.

I lifted my shoulders and sighed. As hard as I'd tried, I couldn't recall one traumatic moment in Buttercup's life—or even his death for that matter.

He'd just seamlessly transitioned from a breathing state to a *not*-breathing state as though it were really no different. Making straight for the bridge with no hesitation, his tail wagging, paws scurrying, as though some wonderful adventure awaited us all.

I placed my hand on his head, combing my fingers through a soft tuft of fur just under his chin, before scratching the spot between his ears. Figuring that if I was connected to all those other souls, connected to the energy of the very ground I knelt upon, then why wouldn't I be connected to Buttercup too?

I concentrated on merging my energy with his, allowing it to stream and meld until I found myself inside his canine head, where I was amazed to see my dog's own personal version of a hellish experience:

The moment he was pulled away from his mama and his five other littermates so he could come live with us.

I admit, the second I saw that, I started to feel angry again, but knowing that came with consequences, I quickly moved past it. Still, what was I supposed to make of that? I mean, really—was he serious? Had he really viewed the move to our house as some kind of wretched experience?

But then I *remembered*.

Remembered how he actually spent that first night—or, should I say, how we *all* spent that first night.

All of us forced to take turns getting out of our beds so that we could try to comfort him as he cried and whimpered and refused to relax.

It was awful.

For us—for him—but probably mostly for him.

He had no way of knowing that the way he felt at that moment wouldn't go on forever.

He had no way of knowing just how good it was about to get.

Though I had no idea how to get that point across to him, had no idea where to even begin.

Thanks to Rebecca and this horrible bubble she'd created, Buttercup was stuck in the one and only truly bad moment he'd ever known, and as far as he was concerned, he'd never known anything else.

So, I did the only thing I could think of—I curled up beside him and continued to scratch that spot between his ears. Trying to fill my mind with vibrant, happy memories of all the fun times we'd shared, hoping they'd somehow find their way into his brain and maybe even carve out a little space for that sweet, quiet *silence* to creep in.

And it wasn't long before the whimpers died down, the whining ceased, and Buttercup lifted his head, popped his eyes open, and jumped to his feet.

Bodhi heaved a big sigh of relief, as I wrapped my arms around my dog and gave him a giant squeeze. Cradling his muzzle with both hands, I peered deep into his big brown eyes to make sure he truly was back.

Then I looked at Bodhi and said, "We have to go find the prince."

But Bodhi was already shaking his head.

Already lifting his arm and pointing toward the very spot where Rebecca now stood.

17

Her dog stood right alongside her, looking nothing like the Snarly Yow/Black Shuck/Hell Beast I remembered from before.

This dog was tiny.

And nervous.

The kind with yippy barks and dancing paws.

While I'd done my best to fill Bodhi in on everything that I'd learned about Rebecca, when we were still searching for Buttercup, while I'd tried to make it clear just how dark and evil she was, one look at his face was all it took to see he wasn't quite sure if he should believe me.

He was conflicted.

Despite all that I'd said, he was so swayed by her sugary-sweet, beribboned exterior he seriously doubted that someone who looked as harmless and fluffy as that was capable of creating a bubble from hell.

Boys.

They are all the same.

All so easily influenced by a bright and shiny saccharine display.

I tensed as she approached, noting the way she made the ground just under her feet transform and bloom into a bouncy, vibrant carpet of green grass with yellow flowering buds that perfectly matched the bow on her dress. Her smile held firm but radiant, her eyes hiding a whole world of secrets I couldn't even begin to guess at, as she thrust forth her hand and offered a tall, sweaty glass filled with some kind of iced murky liquid.

"Thirsty?" she asked, her voice so high-pitched and syrupy, I felt like I'd overdosed on Halloween candy just by listening to it. Prompting me to grab hold of Buttercup, determined to keep him close to my side. Not wanting him to get anywhere near that runty little pooch of hers who could just as easily turn into the worst kind of Hell Beast.

I glanced at Bodhi, seeing the way he looked at her. Carefully observing as though trying to find some kind of middle ground between all the things I'd said, and all the things his eyes were telling him. His brow lowered, eyes narrowed, while his normally bobbing straw paused against his lips, coming to a complete and total standstill.

"Why not give yourself a break and enjoy a little taste.

After all you've been through, you *deserve* it." She pushed the glass toward him and stared deep into his eyes, but Bodhi just continued to stand there, taking her in. His eyes squinted in such a way that I had no way to read them, no way to know what he might've been thinking

"You shouldn't be so hard on yourself, you know. You should trust me when I say I no longer blame you for being so cowardly and caught up in your own fragile image that you made no move to save me."

I squeezed my lids tighter, squeezed till my eyes turned to slits, and though I still couldn't see exactly what he was seeing, I saw enough to know something had changed.

It was the way the air moved and shimmered all around her, making her appear fuzzy and obscured from my view, but still crystal clear to his. And I knew at that instant that, to Bodhi anyway, she looked just like Nicole again.

I grasped for his hand, afraid of losing him to that brand of anguish, but he stepped out of my reach in favor of her. His fingers outstretched, gaze unwavering, reaching for the drink I couldn't allow him to consume.

I thrust my hand between them, determined to keep Bodhi away, the sudden movement alerting her dog and causing it to lower its head, raise its back, and direct a deep, menacing growl right at me.

But before I could intervene, Bodhi had already grabbed it.

Already gripped his fingers around the glass as he stared at Rebecca and said, "You're wasting your time." Knocking the drink so hard it shot clear out of her hand and into the trees. "Your glamour doesn't work on me anymore. You're *not* Nicole. In fact, you're not even close. And just so you know, I've let it all go. I've forgiven myself. Which means you've got no hold over me now that I'm no longer angry."

She tried her best to hide it. I'll give her that. But still, it was clear by the way she tilted her head and lifted her chin, by the way she fluttered her eyes as she gazed over him, that she wasn't quite expecting that.

"Suit yourself." She lifted her small, slim shoulders, allowing the shimmer to fade until she was fully back to being her overdressed self once again. Her eyes flitting toward mine when she added, "How about you, Riley? Would you like a sip?" Her brow rising as her gaze grew dark and deep, she manifested a whole new glass of tea in her hand. "I promise, it's nothing at all like that *false* memory tea the prince served you." She rolled her eyes and shook her dainty head. "You do realize he's crazy, *right*? I mean, you don't actually believe he's a prince, *do you*?" Her lips curled and smirked, as her brow arced in a superior, haughty way.

"First he was one of my father's workers—and not a very good one, I might add. And he was also a *murderer*." She paused with meaning, allowing enough time for her words to fully penetrate. "But *never* a prince, I assure you of that. You know he's responsible for what happened to me, *right*? He's a member of the same group of rebels who planned the revolt. *It's true!*" she urged, reading my gaze and correctly assuming I didn't believe a single word that she'd said. "And you're a fool for both believing him and feeling sorry for him. Not to mention that you're a hypocrite too."

I quirked my brow, curious as to what she could possibly be getting at, and she was all too eager to inform me.

"Murderers get sent to prison all the time, so why is this any different?"

"Because it *is* different." Bodhi jumped to my defense, even though I wasn't really in need of it. "It's not the same at all. You have no right to interfere with any soul's journey—no right at all! And deep down inside, I have a feeling you know that, or you wouldn't be near as defensive as you are."

She bristled. Her eyes practically glowing like her Hell Beast's just had. "You think you know so much—you think you can barge into my turf and push me around just because you both have some kind of weird glow around you?" She gripped the glass so tightly I was sure it would shatter in her hand. Staring us down in a way that made it clear just how truly outraged she was, as though all the ugliness inside was finding its way to the surface. Her hair lifting, becoming crazy, wiry, as her hate shone so bright it took everything I had not to look away.

And I couldn't help but wonder if she truly did believe what she'd said about the prince and her reasons for keeping him and all the other slaves she'd imprisoned, or if that's just the story she told herself so she'd have an excuse to do what she did.

There was only one way to find out.

"You don't know anything!" she screamed, her whole face transforming. "You know nothing—*nothing at all!*"

She continued to carry on like that, raging and shrieking with no end in sight. And feeling more than a little fed up with all the threats and dramatics, and more than a little eager to get to the bottom of it, I looked at her and said, "Fine. I'll see for myself then. Hand it over already." Totally convinced she was little more than an evil, spoiled-rotten brat, but also knowing that there were two sides to every story, and in order to get hers, I had to see it from her point of view.

She stopped, her eyes widening, clearly wondering if it was some kind of trick.

But it was no trick. I was entirely serious. And though Bodhi wasted no time in gripping my arm in warning, well, it was too late.

I was already reaching for the glass.

Already plucking a sparkle from her dress and tossing it in.

Already bringing the brew to my lips.

Already committing to the journey no matter what sort of scene I'd find myself in.

Bodhi's voice a mere trace of an echo as he begged me to stop, begged me not to go through with it.

But it made no difference.

I'd already entered her world.

18

It wasn't at all like I thought.

I mean, not that I can really explain just exactly what I was expecting since it happened so fast I hadn't really allowed myself all that much time to think about it. But still, if I hadn't downed that tea so quickly, if I'd stopped long enough to actually ponder a few things, I don't think I would've envisioned anything even close to the scene in which I found myself.

I was a baby.

No, scratch that. Because actually, Rebecca was the baby, and I was just along for the ride. Observing the events from her point of view, immersed in an event so vivid, so detailed, so real, it was as though I was her.

I could *see* the morning sun eke its way around the scalloped edges of the curtains, as her mother's soft arms encircled me, cradling gently, as she gazed down in the most loving, deeply profound way.

I could *feel* the depths of Rebecca's sorrow, the full range of her confusion, from that very first morning when her mother failed to appear—and all of the mornings that followed—to the moment when it came as no surprise that her first word spoken was "*Mama!*" soon followed by "*Dead*" and then "*Buried.*" The two most often used words to explain the absence of the first.

I grew along with her, transitioning from a crawling baby to a walking child, feeling her body stretch and grow as the soft rolls of baby fat melted away, allowing her to slim down for a time, before she began to blossom into a pretty young girl whose thirteenth year found her with a closet full of sparkly dresses and drawers stuffed with colorful ribbons and bows. Longing for her father to take notice of her, to appreciate the way she looked in them. But he had neither the time nor the interest, viewing his daughter as a nuisance that was best left to the servants to deal with.

And so they did.

So fearful of her father's legacy of anger, they indulged her every whim in hopes she'd never bad-mouth them. Giving her sweets and treats and presents of every kind: a vast array of delicacies she only vaguely desired; a vast array of delicacies they'd long been denied.

It was the recipe for making a monster.

And there was no end in sight.

If there was resentment in their eyes, Rebecca remained unaware of it. She barely paid them any real notice. To her, they had no other purpose than to fulfill her demands—she was sure that was the sole reason for their existence. Her indulgent life had turned her into the kind of brat I'd only seen on reality TV but never once in the reality of real life.

She was a brat of mammoth proportions.

A spoiled-rotten, clueless, friendless girl, who was so firmly entrenched in her fantasy world—one where everything revolved solely around her—she had no idea how awful she'd become.

No idea that the people who served her had not actually asked to be employed by her father.

No idea of the sadistic game of "bowling" he played with those he'd deemed unworthy of a job they didn't even want in the first place.

And yet, I couldn't help but feel sorry for her.

Couldn't help but pity her.

Even though there was no getting around the fact that she was just as beastly as that dog of hers, there was also no denying that she just didn't get it.

Like the prince would say—she was resisting the truth.

And the next thing I knew, she was on the move.

Running so fast I could actually *hear* the huff of her panting breath in my ears, could actually *feel* the moment of confusion when she lost her footing and sprawled across the dirt. Her body hitting so hard, I was jolted even deeper inside her.

So deep, I'd *become* her.

I lifted my face from the ground, snorting out a pile of dirt I'd inhaled while clearing a bunch of small rocks from my mouth.

Spitting and gagging as I struggled to stand, wiping my sleeve hard against my face, then spitting and gagging some more as I paused long enough to look around.

Aware of a voice in my head, urging, *"Move!"*

And though I tried to obey, I was so unused to being her, so unused to having limbs much longer than mine (not to mention the stiff, pouffy dress and tight shoes that were practically binding my feet), it was pretty rough going at first.

But then the voice repeated, adding, *"Hurry! There's no time to waste! They're coming!"*

I stumbled forward, feet fumbling, heart beating frantically, turning toward the house just in time to see a man racing away from the barn, a man I immediately knew was her father, with a confusing array of emotions held in his gaze.

"*Git!*" he yelled, pointing at the house, allowing no time for pleasantries. "Git upstairs and hide in that closet in your mama's old sitting room, and don't come out till I git you myself. Do you hear me?"

I tried to read his gaze, wondering what it was he was hiding from me, but then he said it again, louder this time, and I couldn't help but obey.

"Do *not* come out for anyone but me. No matter what! Now, *git!*" he practically screamed.

I was off. His words trailing behind me as I raced through the front door and up the creaky wooden stairs. The thought of saying good-bye not even entering my mind, since it all seemed surreal, like a game of some kind.

Bad things happened to other people, not me.

I was rich, privileged, the only child of a big, important, plantation owner, which made me special in a way that far surpassed all the others. Aside from my mother's untimely death, anything negative, dreary, or bad had always whizzed past me on its way toward somebody else.

I made for my mama's old sitting room, just like my papa had ordered. And though I was sure no one knew, the truth is, I'd often visited that room.

I liked to sit in the soft, cushy upholstered chair she used for reading, before switching to the less comfortable straight-backed one she used for correspondence and list making. And more often than not, I'd play either one of two games: one in which I pretended she was still here, reading and chatting with me, and another in which I'd somehow become her, found a way to stand in her place.

But today there was no time for games.

Soon enough my papa would climb the stairs and come find me. And when he did, well, I was eager for him to see just how perfect I was.

Just how willingly I'd obeyed his every word.

Then maybe he'd finally take notice of me, since he never seemed to notice before.

I made for the closet, crawled into the small, dark, rarely used space, wrapped my fingers around the edge of the door and pulled it shut as well as I could. Crouching all the way against the back wall, just about all settled in, when I remembered my dog.

I scooched forward, propped the door open, peeked my head out, and called, "Shucky! Here, boy!" before chasing that with a low, even whistle I prayed my father wouldn't hear.

Relieved by the sound of Shucky's paws scurrying across the wood floors, I caught him as he slipped inside the closet and jumped right onto my lap. Yipping softly, he excitedly lapped at my cheeks, as I shut the door again and moved us back into place.

I clutched him to my chest and tried not to giggle at the way his icy-cold nose prodded against my shoulder and neck. Struggling to ignore the cloying scent of mold and mustiness and various things that hadn't been used in a very long time, while I worked to decipher the look I'd seen in my father's eyes.

Was it love that I'd seen?

And would I even recognize it if it was?

It'd been so long since anyone looked upon me that way, I had no way to recognize the signs.

And that's how I spent my last moments.

Fending off old closet smells, fending off my dog's stale, panting breath, while trying to determine just exactly what my father's gaze had meant.

My legs beginning to ache from being so awkwardly bent, my back and buttocks growing sore from leaning for so long against the hardwood floor.

Wondering if I should maybe take a quick peek, see what might be taking him so long to find me, when my dog suddenly stiffened, perked up his ears, and narrowed his eyes as he let out a low, menacing growl.

But while he may have been the first to sense it, it wasn't long till there was no mistaking it.

The sound of a stampede—hundreds of bodies running with purpose.

The sound of violence—things crashing and breaking as a series of screams rang out, one in particular, one that I recognized as my father's, that rose above all the rest.

The sound of my front door being pulled from its hinges.

The sound of my house being stormed, invaded, ransacked, and looted.

The sound of the horrible, lingering silence of a papa that never came looking for me.

And yet, I continued to wait like he asked.

Waited long past the time the crackling began and the closet floors began to heat.

Long past the time gray ribbons of smoke curled their way in and around the door frame and rendered it impossible to breathe.

Long past the time the flames licked at my heels and rose up my dress like snakes.

Long past the time my frightened dog clawed huge gaping holes in my dress as he fought with all of his might to escape.

But I wouldn't let him go, wouldn't let him leave without me, I just held him fast to my chest, my lips incessantly whispering my father's warning:

Do not come out for anyone but me, no matter what!

My body blistering and burning, as the bow on my dress worked like some kind of accelerant and encouraged the flames to leap onto my hair and my face. Engulfing me in a pain so wrenching, so great, I told myself it was a game.

That it couldn't possibly be happening to someone as special as me.

Repeating the words as a wave of red, searing-hot timbers crashed down upon us, reducing my dog and me to nothing more than a pile of charred bones and black dust.

Obedient till the end, I'd died in the exact location where my father had told me to wait.

Then, just as quickly, I was *out*.

Gazing down at what little remained of myself and my dog as the scene continued to play, seeing smoke, fire, destruction, and blood, most of which belonged to my father, judging from the looks of his severely mangled body.

And when I saw what had caused it or, rather, *who* had caused it—when I realized we'd all been murdered—well, from that moment on, all I could see was red.

A bright, raging red that shimmered and glowed and bubbled all around until it was big enough to house me.

Anger.

All I could feel—all I could *see*—was a burning hot *anger* that raged deep inside me.

An anger so intense it came to define me.

And so I vowed my revenge, vowed that every single one of them would pay for making me like this.

Ignoring the vague, magnetic pull of something bright and promising and good—preferring to spend the rest of my days in my angry new world.

I watched the massacre continue, lasting just over a month, watched as the death toll and bodies all piled up. Allowing those I'd deemed innocent to follow that pull to whatever bright thing lay beyond, while luring the rest of them into my shimmering trap of revenge— watching it grow bigger and bigger with each and every soul I admitted, until it became the large, dark globe where we lived.

My throat grew dry and constricted, and for someone who no longer breathes, I had the sensation of desperately needing to before I was suffocated. The weight of Rebecca's soul becoming so heavy, so burdensome, I couldn't even begin to describe my relief when I found myself back on the other side of it.

I coughed and sputtered, and tried my best to center myself. And even though Bodhi patted my back and Buttercup softly licked my hand, it took a while till I was able to face them again.

When I did, I looked right at Rebecca and said, "I'm sorry for what happened to you." I fought to keep my voice steady, sincere. "But I'm also sorry to tell you that you're wrong. *Dead wrong.* Every thing you're doing here and all of your reasons behind it are way off. You are sorely misguided, and too many people are suffering because of it."

But even though I tried to gaze upon her with love and compassion, I guess I didn't really realize until it was way past too late that the look, the word, and the emotion was completely unrecognizable, completely meaningless, to someone like her.

The next thing I knew, little Shucky had transformed into the Hell Beast I'd first met, as Rebecca stood before us, shaking with uncontrollable rage, her eyes glowing in the same way as her dog's.

"You will *never* leave this place!" she screamed. "You will never find your way out of here! *Never,* I swear it!"

The ground shook, the wind howled, and a steaming hot blaze flared and burned all around, and less than a second later, Rebecca and her Hell Beast were gone.

19

I will never forget the sound of it.

For as long as I continue to exist, I know for a fact that that sound will exist right along with me.

I mean, how do you get past the shriek of hundreds of souls screaming in agony?

How can you possibly get over something like that?

Just because they were no longer encased in real, physical, flesh-and-blood bodies—just because they were no longer in possession of a beating heart and central nervous system—didn't mean they were aware of that.

Rebecca ruled their perception in a way that made all of their mental and physical agonies seem all too real, just as she continued to rule our reality too.

The gale raged around us, whipping my hair into a frenzy, causing it to lash hard against my face, leaving me with no choice but to duck my head low, squint my eyes tightly, and yell into the howl of the wind. My voice rough, hoarse, as I struggled to be heard over the blare, warning Bodhi and Buttercup to concentrate, to locate the small gap of *silence* in their own heads, reminding them as well as myself that it was the only way to keep us from sinking even deeper into Rebecca's hell.

Yet, despite all of that, despite the fact that we all knew better, it was pretty rough going for each of us. It was one thing to know we were playing into the false reality of Rebecca's world—quite another to spare ourselves from it.

I manifested a leash for Buttercup, something he usually hates, but at that moment he was all too willing to be anchored to me, and we clung to each other, making our way between souls, our bodies getting battered and buffeted as we desperately searched for the prince. But there was so much wind, and smoke, and debris, so many traumatized souls, it was impossible to see his.

"We have to split up." Bodhi grasped my arm and shouted into my ear. "I know you don't want to, but trust me, it's the only way. We have to free these souls one by one. If we stay like this and do nothing, we'll never get anywhere. We'll just get sucked into the vortex of extreme suffering, along with the rest of them."

I looked at him, not at all sure if I was really up for the task. Even though I felt like I knew the territory, possibly better than him, there was still a small part of me that didn't trust myself.

There was still a small part of me that didn't quite believe I could actually, effectively accomplish all that.

I was barely handling myself *with* them, so how could I possibly maintain my concentration and focus without them?

I mean, it's one thing to talk the talk—it's quite another to actually walk it.

And as far as I and focusing went, well, let's just say we were like two distant cousins that'd rarely met.

But Bodhi, sensing, if not hearing, my hesitation, along with every worried thought in my head, looked at me and said, "You can do it, Riley. You're going to be fine. Heck, you helped me, didn't you?"

I nodded. That much was true, though the reminder didn't do much to ease my own nagging doubt.

"And what about Buttercup? Where would he be right now if it wasn't for you?"

I gazed down at my dog, who was gazing up at me, and I couldn't help but hope he couldn't hear my thoughts just like I couldn't hear his. I didn't want him to know what a big wimp I'd become.

I wrapped my arms around my waist and bent my head low, my hair whipping all around me, getting thrashed pretty good, as I danced around on my tippy toes to keep my feet from being burned.

Some apprentice I was turning out to be—I couldn't even concentrate my way past Rebecca's manifested weather storm.

I'd barged my way in here without ever once stopping to consider just what I might be getting myself into only to flip out and lose all my nerve at the exact moment it truly began to matter.

It was like gazing into a mirror and seeing the absolute very worst version of me.

But then again, I was only twelve.

Eternally stuck at twelve.

And with that in mind, how much could really be expected of me?

It's not like being dead made me any wiser than I'd been when I was alive.

It's not like being dead made me any more mature, or instilled any more confidence or strength in me than I'd had on my very last day on the earth plane.

I mean, maybe if I'd been allowed to make it to *thirteen*, I'd be grown-up enough to face something like this. But, as it was, thirteen, and all that it promised, was never going to happen for me, so why should I be expected to deal with something as big as all this?

But just after I'd finished the thought, Bodhi tugged hard on my sleeve and said, "You're wrong."

I raised my head slightly and peered at him through my tangled up bangs.

"You *can* concentrate and focus, you've already proved that."

I swallowed hard. Even though my body no longer made saliva that I could actually swallow, I did it anyway. Old habits really do die hard, it seems.

"Not to mention the fact that you don't know squat about the Here & Now."

He had my full attention.

"You have no idea how it works, do you?" Bodhi asked.

My eyes locked on his.

"No one is ever *stuck* anywhere, Riley. Seriously, what kind of a place do you think it is?"

I looked at him, because to be honest, I really wasn't sure. At that point, I still had a whole lot of questions as to how it all worked.

He ducked his head lower and clenched that green straw between his teeth as he said, "Then again, I guess now you'll never find out just what you're truly capable of over there. You know, since you're choosing to be *stuck* here instead."

I gaped, at first unable to utter the words, though it wasn't long before I said, "You mean, I can . . . I can, maybe . . .

actually . . . *turn thirteen someday*?" I pressed my lips together, sure it was too good to be true.

But Bodhi just quirked his brow and shrugged in a vague, noncommittal kind of way. "There're no limits that I'm aware of—pretty much anything is possible there. But, the sad part is you'll never even get close if you can't find your way out of here."

I stared down at my toes, my dancing scorched toes. Hearing his voice in my head urging, "*Concentrate. Focus.* See the *true reality* of this place, not the one Rebecca wants you to see."

So I did.

And it wasn't long before the wind stopped, the fire extinguished, the ground went still, and my toes cooled, though my hair still looked like a fright wig.

"You can deal with that later." Bodhi laughed, chucking me under my chin. "But first, we have some souls to release."

20

Buttercup and I went one way, while Bodhi went another. Each of us approaching the nearest, suffering soul, taking hold of their hand, and immersing ourselves in their world of pain until we could introduce that small space of *silence* that guided them out of their hell.

And if you think that sounds simple, if you think that sounds easy-peasy, well, let me tell you it isn't.

Not even close.

The truth is, we were subjected to some pretty dark things—along with some pretty scary things, and some pretty horrific things, and some pretty sad things. And I'll speak for myself when I say I personally witnessed the kind of suffering I never could've imagined, never *wanted* to imagine, before.

I *felt* the crack of the whip against my bare back that caused my skin to break open and ooze.

I *watched* with an indescribable fear as an intentionally aimed bowling ball whizzed right past my face, missing me by only a fraction of an inch.

I heard the horrible *thwonk* as that same bowling ball slammed into a far less fortunate friend, filled with the horrifying knowledge that yet another brother had passed.

But still, I kept right on going, offering hope, love, and compassion—the three biggest, most powerful forces in the universe—and when I saw that moment of reprieve, when I saw that small gap of silence introduced, well, I encouraged them to seize it, focus on it, and grow it until it became big enough for them to climb into.

Big enough for them to fly away in.

And somewhere along the way, a funny thing happened.

With every soul we released, Rebecca's world, her darkly glistening bubble of anger, grew a little bit smaller.

Though I couldn't see her, I could tell by the way Buttercup stilled, lowered his head, and pulled in his tail, that Rebecca was somewhere among us. But for the time being anyway, she didn't dare approach, and honestly, I felt so empowered by the work I was doing, I'm not sure I would've cared if she had.

Suddenly, I had something that was missing before: a strong belief in myself and the promise of a future I hadn't dared to even think about.

Because if what Bodhi said was true, I just might get to experience my biggest dream yet: that of being *thirteen*.

But first, we had some serious business to attend to.

Each soul was different. No two were alike. Some were angry with themselves, some were angry with others, while some had lived lives so horrendous it was truly impossible to fathom.

Still, I wasn't there to judge: I was merely there to provide some relief. So I continued to make my way through the ranks, thinning the crowd significantly, until I stopped to take a good look around and was amazed to find the world had been dwindled down to Bodhi, Buttercup, Prince Kanta, and me.

To say I was thrilled to see the prince again would be putting it mildly. Though I'd tried not to think too much about it, tried to stay focused on the soul at hand, I'd be lying if I said I hadn't been pretty disturbed by his absence.

But when I tried to introduce him to Bodhi, I realized they'd run into each other just a little earlier, around the time the walls really started to close in and they'd bumped right into each other.

And though none of us actually said it, I knew we were all looking for Rebecca. Her world had shrunk to the point where there was only one place left to hide—in the big yellow house, a manifested replica of the one she grew up in.

I stared at the mansion, unsure if we should make the first move to go get her or wait for her to come to her senses, acknowledge her defeat, and find her way outside to wave her white flag.

But when Bodhi mentioned tearing the house down in order to get to her, I had another idea.

I slipped right in front of them and made my way in, swiftly ascending the stairs with my friends right behind me, knowing exactly where I'd find her since I'd already lived the experience.

I went straight for the closet. And while I admit, for a split second I considered manifesting some kind of facade that looked just like her father, knowing that would certainly lure her right out, in the end, I decided against it. Partly because it just didn't seem right—it seemed cruel and unkind—and partly because I really had no idea how to do that (though I made a mental note to ask later).

I paused before the door, glancing over my shoulder to see the prince and Bodhi nodding their encouragement, while Buttercup thumped his tail against the floor.

Then I grabbed hold of the knob and yanked the door open, my eyes narrowing as they adjusted to the dim, spying nothing more than the tips of her shiny brown boots, the hem of her flouncy dress, and the stray paw of the dog she clutched to her chest, until I moved all the old hanging clothes aside and could gaze upon the rest of her.

Our eyes met. And for a moment, I was sure I couldn't go through with it. But the thought was quickly overcome by something I can only describe as a *thought wave*—this big, wonderful swarm of love and support that came from my friends.

Strengthened by the way it swept right over me, pooled all around me, I looked at Rebecca and said, "It's over. *Everything's* over. You're the only one left, and now it's time to come out."

But if I'd had any illusions it would be anywhere near that easy, well, I quickly got over them.

Rebecca wasn't going anywhere. And somewhere in the midst of all her yelling and cursing and ranting and raving, she'd told me as much.

"He's not coming," I said, deflecting each verbal blow, letting it just whiz right past me. "Your father is *gone*. He moved on a long time ago. Which means there's really no point in reliving all this."

She scooched back even further, clutched her dog tighter, and kicked at me with her boots. And when it was clear I wasn't going anywhere, when it was clear that none of us were, she did the unthinkable.

She let go of her dog and sicked him on Buttercup.

I screamed.

I couldn't help it.

The sight of that *beast* charging my dog caused me to lose all my focus.

But luckily, I had backup.

Backup that wasn't the least bit fazed by any of it.

And no, I'm not referring to Bodhi, or even Prince Kanta as I definitely heard them suck in a fair amount of air—I'm talking about Buttercup.

My sweet yellow Lab, who, seeing the dog now grown to one hundred times his size, equated it with the game of fetch he'd been playing earlier, the game that started all this. Manifesting a lime green tennis ball, just like the one we'd been using, he sent it bouncing toward the door, down the hall, then barked and wagged his tail harder as he watched the hellhound chase after it.

The last thing I heard as Shucky ran down the stairs and out the front door was the sound of Rebecca scream-ing, *"Nooooooo!"* When she realized her dog, thanks to mine, was now on the other side of her globe.

We tried to cajole her, tried to convince her to join him, but she refused. Even after we'd stripped away the closet, the house, and tried to show her just how quickly her world had shrunk down, that besides the three of us, she was the only inhabitant left, she still resisted the truth.

Choosing to fight back by manifesting all manner of

hateful, anger-making memories along with every natural disaster she could think of.

But we remained calm, and focused and united—each of us happily residing in the small, quiet space of *silence* she could no longer take from us.

"What now?" I glanced between the prince and Bodhi, looking for some wise words, if not guidance.

"We leave her." The prince shrugged. "Now that my brothers and sisters are freed"—he nodded toward the place just outside the globe where they all stood, peering in at us—"it is time for me to go. I was hoping to reach her, but that does not seem to be possible just yet. And for that, I am sorry. It is a very great failure on my part."

Though Bodhi was quick to agree that we should all just leave and possibly revisit that sad, angry girl on some other day, I had another idea entirely.

"I know *exactly* how to get her out of here," I said, looking at each of them. "Just follow my lead."

21

"You can't do it," Bodhi said, but I turned my back on him, determined to go through with it no matter how he might choose to protest. "You cannot force someone to cross the bridge. It goes against all the rules. And I can't believe I have to repeat this to you when you already know that."

I glanced at the prince, embarrassed to be bickering in front of him like this. Still, I had every intention to stand my ground. I'd had an idea. A good one, if I might say so myself. And I was sure it would work if Bodhi would just give it half a chance.

"No one's *forcing* anyone to do anything," I said, making it a point to roll my eyes and shake my head. "I mean, *sheesh*, whaddaya take me for? Some kind of amateur?" I screwed my lips to the side.

"Then what?" he asked, voice still full of the fight.

"You can *see* she's not cooperating, so short of *forcing* her to do what you want, how are you going to possibly convince her?"

I clutched my hips and gazed all around, just because he was in charge of guiding me, didn't mean he knew squat when it came to the depths of my imagination. "I'm not going to *force* her, and I seriously doubt I'll be able to *convince* her—though I do know something that will."

Bodhi squinted, taking his annoyance out on the straw he mangled hard between his teeth.

"The *bridge* will convince her."

He sighed. One of those big, loud, exasperated kind of sighs that was soon followed by, "Excuse me, but did I not just tell you that—" But his words were cut short by the flash of my hand.

"Maybe you're right," I said, gazing between him and the prince. "Maybe I can't *force* her to cross it, but that doesn't mean I can't lead her to it."

They looked at me.

"And once she sees the promise it holds, well, there's no way she can resist."

"Yeah? And what if she does?" Bodhi asked, stubbornly refusing to see the absolute genius of my plan.

But I just shrugged. "Well, then I guess we'll cross it, and leave her to stare at it for the rest of eternity. But there's no way it'll come to that," I said, my voice bearing far more conviction than I actually felt.

"So how do you propose we get her there, to this . . . *bridge*?" the prince asked, still dressed in the rags he wore when we first met.

I dropped my hands to my sides and squinted at her—the world she'd created, the one that once seemed so large and overwhelming, only to be reduced to the size of an average thirteen-year-old girl.

She glared at us, all of us. Her fists raised in anger, shouting every type of threat she could think of. And she was so furious to see her little dog Shucky (back to being the tiny version of himself), sitting right alongside Buttercup that she even included him in those threats.

To be honest, if you'd asked me at that moment how I planned to get her anywhere even close to that bridge, well, I really couldn't have said. I mean, it's not like the journey was all that long, since all we had to do was make the soft golden veil of light and slip through it to the other side, but still, how would we get *her* through it?

How would we lead her first to Summerland, and then, hopefully, to the Here & Now just beyond?

Then it hit me—why not just *roll* her there?

After all, the bubble was perfectly round, which should make it easy enough. And though I knew she wouldn't like it, by that point, I admit, I wasn't really all that concerned about that.

I approached the globe, placed my hands on either side of the space where her eyes glowed and her cheeks flamed bright red, and I started to push. Rolling her slowly at first, seeing her tumble and fall and totally freak as her whole world was sent upside down and a crazy swirl of ash sprayed all over the place.

And just as I was about to deem it a somewhat awkward, but still overall, success, one of Prince Kanta's *brothers,* a former slave whom I recognized from that sadistic bowling game of Rebecca's father, placed his hand on my arm, and when our eyes met, what I saw practically brought me to my knees.

And I watched in amazement, as he took my place, knelt down to the ground, and attempted to lift the bubble right onto his back.

At first I didn't understand the gesture. Didn't understand why he'd chosen to burden himself like that. But then, when all of the other slaves joined in, it suddenly began to make sense.

They had *forgiven* her.

They had *released* themselves not just from her manifested world but also from their centuries-long connection to her.

By holding on to their anger, hatred, and calls for revenge, they'd remained enslaved well past the time of their deaths.

Their true liberation, their true path to freedom, lay in their ability to forgive.

A forgiveness that didn't absolve Rebecca or her father of the horrible things they had done, but rather freed the slaves of their connection to those horrible things, as well as their connection to those who'd committed them, allowing them to finally move on.

Then, just when I was sure I'd seen it all, Prince Kanta shocked me even more when he said, "Allow me."

And a moment later, he'd manifested a beautiful, luxurious litter—like the kind Cleopatra rode—and together, they placed the globe upon it, immune to the sight of Rebecca kicking and screaming and sending great plumes of ash all around. As a whole group of former slaves stepped forward to grab hold of the shiny, golden rail that ran along its sides, as Bodhi and I joined hands, closed our eyes, and manifested that soft, golden light that leads to Summerland.

The two of us standing back in awe, watching as the very people who were enslaved by Rebecca and her father carried her right through that veil in what I will forever carry in my head as the ultimate picture of *forgiveness*.

22

When we got to Summerland, they lowered the litter onto that vibrant, buoyant grass. Each of the slaves taking a moment to place their hands on the glass and leave her with a blessing of peace, before Prince Kanta stepped forward to say, "You have liberated my brothers and sisters. Because of you, Miss Riley Bloom, they are now freed not only from their physical enslavement but, more importantly, from the enslavement of their own minds. I speak on behalf of all of us when I say that we are eternally grateful to you for showing the way."

I quickly shook my head, fought to work past that choked-up feeling in my throat, and glanced down the long line of them as I said, "I only introduced them to that glimmer of silence, they grew it from there."

Even though I meant it, even though I knew they'd truly done the hardest work of all—quieting their minds of all the anger and hatred and judging and chaos, along with their very justified rage regarding their own horrific pasts—I still couldn't help but feel a little bit proud of myself.

I also couldn't wait to get in front of a mirror to see how an act like that might've affected my glow.

But that would have to wait till later. Much later. At that point, I still had a whole lot of souls to cross over.

So when Prince Kanta peered from me to the bridge—a rather ancient, rickety-looking, splintered-wood-and-rope contraption—I just nodded and said, "Yep, that's it. Paradise awaits you on the other side. Only they don't call it paradise, they call it the Here & Now—but, anyway, you'll learn about all that soon enough."

"And Rebecca?" he asked, turning back toward the globe. "Will she ever find the peace to free herself?"

But I just shrugged. I had no answer for that. It was pretty much anyone's guess.

He motioned for the group to go before him, and after shaking my and Bodhi's hands, after kneeling down to pat Buttercup and Shucky on their heads, they squared their shoulders, lifted their chins, straightened their backs, and made for the bridge in what looked to be a seemingly endless procession.

And even though I knew there would be plenty more souls to catch in the future, even though I knew I'd soon rack up all kinds of interesting assignments, in possibly even more exotic locations than St. John Virgin Islands, somehow I knew that this would always stand out in my mind.

Not because I'd insisted on exercising my freewill and going it alone.

Not because I'd had no idea how it would go over with Aurora and Royce and the rest of the Council (something I hadn't really stopped worrying about despite the success of my mission).

But because there was a really good chance I might never again witness something as powerful.

And as they continued their march, the bridge swaying and dipping but still strong enough to hold them all, making their way past the heavily fogged and shrouded halfway mark, this particular part of Summerland, an area that was always wet and misty and shrouded in haze became as bright and warm as any spring day back home on the earth plane.

It actually began to *glow*.

I turned to the prince, seeing him hesitate, gazing at Rebecca with great concern as she continued to scream and rant and rave. And what bothered me most about seeing her carrying on like that was I knew it made the prince feel like he'd failed.

"This is *not* good," I whispered to Bodhi. "I really

thought she might come around once she saw this place, but, apparently, she's more far gone than I thought."

But Bodhi just looked at me, straw bobbing up and down in his mouth as he mumbled, "Maybe."

I squinted, having no idea what that was supposed to mean.

"It means, *we'll see.*" He shrugged, clearly taking advantage of the fact that his thoughts were completely unavailable to me.

I focused back on the former slaves, and as soon as the last one had crossed, I watched in complete and total astonishment as Bodhi reached toward the former Snarly Yow/Black Shuck/Phantom Dog/Galleytrot/Shug Monkey/Hateful Thing/Hell Beast-turned-tiny-yippy breed of indeterminate mix, grabbed the ball that lay at his feet, and aimed it straight toward the bridge. Smiling in triumph as it pierced through the haze that obscured the middle and little Shucky went yapping and yipping, and chasing right after it.

"Hey! That's cheating!" I cried, gaping at him in complete disbelief. "I can't believe you did that—I can't believe you *forced* him like that."

But Bodhi just looked at me, shaking his head as he said, "No one *forced* anyone. That dog acted upon his own *freewill.* He *chose* to go after that ball, just like you chose to exercise your freewill when you chose to go after him." He bobbed his straw at me. "Freewill is a powerful thing, Riley. Sometimes it's the only way to realize your true destiny, though it does require a fair bit of trust—in yourself, in the universe—as I'm sure you now know."

I nodded, carefully collecting his words and storing them away for later. Knowing I'd want to go over them, review them, but at that moment, all of my attention was claimed by Rebecca.

Claimed by the way her jaw dropped, the way her eyes went impossibly wide, the way her face wore an expression of both outrage and surprise as she watched her dog happily sprint to the other side.

"Where'd he go?" she asked, her anger edged out by wonder.

"He went *home*," I said quietly, looking right at her. "And you're welcome to join him if you want. The choice is yours."

She glanced between us, and the way she looked at that moment, well, all I can say is I was filled with hope for her for the first time that day.

I mean, don't get me wrong, she still looked a little red around the cheeks, a little grim around the lips, but still, it was pretty clear that the fight was beginning to leak right out of her.

She stood facing us, locked inside a world she'd already spent far too much time in. Her fingers beginning to unclench, her hands to uncurl, as she stared into the glowing golden promise of light and whispered, "Oh my goodness . . . it's *all* true!"

I admit, I totally misread that at first.

I was sure she was referring to the light, to paradise, the Here & Now, whatever you prefer to call it. It was an awesome sight, and once witnessed, the pull was nearly impossible to resist.

But I was wrong.

As it turns out, it was even better than that.

Rebecca wasn't just referring to that awesome golden glow—she was referring to the *truth* she'd seen residing inside it.

A truth she'd resisted for so many years, centuries really, that was now projecting in a way that couldn't be missed.

She saw the truth of her life—and that of Prince Kanta's as well. But despite her horrible, selfish acts, she also saw it wasn't the grim place of punishment she secretly feared.

It was a place of love and warmth and understanding of the deepest kind.

It was a place where she'd never again feel so alone as she had in her life.

She also saw the dim outline of her mother, waiting for her at the halfway mark.

And the next thing I knew, her entire world shattered.

Her globe broke.

Her bubble burst.

As a hail of glasslike shards flew about, hovering in the air for a moment in a way that resembled a shimmering blanket of stars, before softly falling to the ground, where they landed at her feet and melted into the grass.

She moved toward the prince, and I couldn't help but tense, but then Bodhi put his hand on my arm, Buttercup nudged up beside me, and I began to calm again. And just when I was sure she was going to curtsy before him in the way she'd done with me, she did something entirely different.

Something I wasn't expecting.

She knelt all the way down to her knees and rested her head at his feet in the ultimate act of humility.

Refusing to rise again until the prince gently urged, "Child, please. It is not necessary."

He reached for her hand and helped her to stand until she was once again facing him. Only this time her rage was all gone, having dissolved with the bubble and leaving a very sorry, very humbled young girl in its place.

"I am *so* very sorry," she said, her voice faint, tremulous, "for what I've done to you—for what my father did to you . . ." She shook her head and winced at a memory she'd denied for centuries. Finally able to see the truth of *everything*—of every horrible act committed against him—and I knew at that moment that the old Rebecca had gone and a new one had taken her place. "I have no idea how I'll ever make it up to you, but I promise I will. I'll do whatever it takes, just tell me where to begin."

Her eyes and cheeks glistened, as a stream of crystalline tears spilled down her face. And I watched in amazement as the prince leaned forward, caught one of those tears on the tip of his finger, and turned it into a beautiful olive branch.

"There is no need." He placed the branch onto her outstretched hands. "I forgave you long ago. I was just waiting for you to rid yourself of your anger. Believe me when I say that the physical suffering I endured as a slave was nothing compared to the suffering of the bubble when I was tortured by my own mind, my own memories of the horrible things that'd been done to me, as well as the horrible things I had done to others." He paused, making sure she understood, before he offered his arm and said, "So, what do you say? Shall we?"

She nodded softly and entwined her arm around his, the two of them stopping before us, as Rebecca looked at me and said, "I'm so sorry, I—"

But I just flashed my palm and stopped her right there. "No worries," I told her. "Trust me, this is hardly good-bye.

The Here & Now may be a pretty big place, but I'm sure I'll see you again. I'll just look for the girl with the bright yellow bow and the sparkly dress."

She gazed down at herself, clearly embarrassed to wear such attire while the prince was in rags.

And so he immediately manifested a new tunic for himself, while she took the opportunity to change into something a little less gaudy, a little more drab.

Then after shaking hands and hugging, and saying what turned out to be a pretty tearful good-bye, I started to turn away, sure it was really, truly over, when they reached the foot of the bridge and the prince turned to say, "Miss Riley!"

I glanced over my shoulder, meeting his gaze, and, well, let's just say, that's when I finally reached the second goal I had made.

Not only had I broken down that bubble and ushered all those lost souls toward their true intended destinies, but because of it, the prince had rewarded me with the most warm and wonderful full-on, white-toothed, dimple-inducing smile.

"What's that about?" Bodhi asked, glancing between us.

But I just shrugged, smiling and waving good-bye to the prince as I said, "Trust me, you wouldn't understand."

23

The second they were gone, Bodhi looked at me and said, "So what now? You still want to finish your vacation? We never did check out the town."

But I just shook my head. As far as I was concerned, my little *vacay* was o-v-e-r. No matter how cool that town was reputed to be, no way could it hold a candle to the places I'd been.

I'd just experienced the kind of amazing St. John adventure that could never be found in any brochure, which pretty much guaranteed that anything that followed would only pale in comparison.

"So what, then?" He crouched down to pet Buttercup, while still gazing at me. "You wanna go somewhere else? The Council's not expecting us back any time soon, which means we can pretty much do whatever we want."

I narrowed my gaze, drummed my fingers hard against

my hips, and took a little time to analyze what he'd just said.

Why was he trying so hard to keep me at a party that was so clearly over?

Was he baiting me?

Trying to trick me by seeing if I'd choose lingering in St. John over heading back to the Here & Now and face the repercussions for taking on a job that hadn't been assigned to me?

Or, was he serious about continuing the vacation?

And if so, for what reason?

Was it so we could continue to get to know each other better?

Because, quite frankly, after experiencing what it was like to *be* him during that whole scene with Nicole, I was pretty much feeling like I knew him better than I ever wanted to, *thankyouverymuch*.

And, I have to say, the longer I pondered, the more of a conundrum I found myself in—one in which I was, yet again, torn between both the more rational and paranoid sides of me.

"Let's go," I said, nodding firmly so he'd know I was serious. "Let's just make our way back."

He looked at me, his eyes gone all squinty as he made some totally disgusting slurping sound with his straw.

"Seriously. I mean, we're almost there anyway, so why delay any further?"

And the way he looked at me, well, let's just say it was so revealing, I couldn't help but realize that Bodhi wasn't actually baiting *me* per se—it was more like he was baiting himself *through* me.

He was the one who didn't want to return.

He was the one who was afraid to go before the Council.

After everything we'd just accomplished, which was pretty dang major if I do say so myself, he was feeling pretty insecure about how it might go over—doubting the Council would view it in his favor.

After all, his job was to guide me, and if you think about it in its most basic terms, it was pretty clear he'd totally failed on that one.

He'd tried to guide me toward *not* going after the Hell Beast. But did I listen? Of course not! I just willfully went off on my own, leaving him with no choice but to chase me down, and even so, once he caught up with me, he still couldn't stop me—he'd had no choice but to follow *my* lead.

The thought alone made me feel bad.

Maybe even a tiny bit ashamed of myself.

Clearly, I was just as difficult to guide in my death as I had been in life.

I was still stubborn, still impulsive, still impatient—I

was all the awful things he'd accused me of being and more.

It was as though *nothing* had changed—or at least nothing having to do with my personality anyway.

And yet, as he himself said earlier, I'd had every right to exercise my freewill.

And no one, not even my guide, could rob me of that.

"Let's go," I repeated, glancing over my shoulder to see Buttercup running, trying to catch up with me. "We can fly, we can walk, we can ignore the bridge and take the long, scenic route if you want. I'll leave that up to you. In the end, it all leads back to the same place. It all leads back home."

24

By the time we got back to the Here & Now, Bodhi seemed pretty eager to be rid of me.

I didn't even get so much as a *good-bye, see ya later, adios, nothing*, before he was well on his way.

"Um, hel-*lo*!" I called, narrowing my eyes on his retreating back and shaking my head. "Aren't you forgetting a little something called *the Council*?" Sure, he was trying to avoid what I knew to be inevitable.

He stopped, spun on his heel, and looked right at me. "*We* don't approach the Council, Riley, the Council approaches *us*."

Oh.

I gazed down at the ground, feeling painfully aware that for all my bravado on the earth plane, I was still pretty incompetent Here.

"So, how will I know when it's time?" I asked, feeling

kind of stupid for asking, but how else was I supposed to learn?

But Bodhi just looked at me. "They'll summon me, and then I'll summon you." He gazed all around, as though he had somewhere urgent to be. "So—are we through here?" he asked, never more eager to get away from me.

I nodded, watching him retreat again, and having to physically restrain Buttercup from going after him.

Traitor! I'd started to say as I glared down at my dog, the word melting fast on my tongue the second he gazed up at me with those big brown eyes.

Still, it's not like I could blame him for preferring Bodhi over me. From what I'd seen, Bodhi was like the rock star of this place. In fact, he probably had a whole slew of groupies and friends, an entire entourage of fans just waiting to catch up with him, while I just had me.

Okay, maybe that's not exactly true.

Maybe I had my parents and my grandparents too.

But still, as nice as it was to know they were out there, somewhere, it still couldn't compare to the kind of friendships I longed for.

The kind I'd had back on the earth plane.

The kind that came with laughs and good times and a shared interest in a lot, if not all, the same things.

And to be honest, not only was I totally confused by the

way things worked Here, but I was so bad at controlling what could only be described as my overly judgmental, superficial thoughts and opinions that apparently everyone could hear, that I didn't even know how to go about making any friends.

So I wandered. Telling myself it would help me get the lay of the land, though the truth is, deep down inside, I knew it was a lie.

I knew exactly where I was headed, which meant it came as no surprise when I ended up just outside the Viewing Room.

Even though I knew it was discouraged, if not downright frowned upon—even though I knew it would disappoint my parents, the Council, and probably Bodhi as well, even though my dog stopped just shy of it, refusing to be an accomplice and go any further, gazing up at me with an *Oh, no she didn't* kind of gaze—I ducked in anyway.

Grabbing a number from the dispenser and taking my place in what turned out to be a pretty long line, lying to myself yet again when I vowed I'd just take a quick peek, check in on my sister and maybe a few old friends, and then be on my way.

I waited my turn, checking out all the blue hairs, many of whom I recognized from my last illicit visit, and I couldn't help but wonder why it was okay for them to look in on the earth plane, but not me?

Was it because they all claimed to be merely checking in on their grandkids, as opposed to salaciously watching the goings-on as though it were some kind of live-action soap opera like I did?

Or was there some kind of Here & Now double standard that allowed only the geriatrics to get all nostalgic, while the young ones were urged to forget?

The line grew as I inched my way closer to the front. Determined to keep to myself, to mind my own business, when I heard some old guy behind me say, "She still worries about me. After all this time, she just won't stop grieving. No matter how many times I visit her in her dreams, no matter how many times I take her hand and say, 'Helen, listen to me, I promise you, I am A-OK. Now please—get back to living!' as soon as she wakes up, she convinces herself it wasn't really me, and the grief starts again. And sometimes"—he paused, as I took a moment to surreptitiously check out the shiny black dress shoes and matching black socks he wore with his plaid Bermuda shorts—"I tell ya, Mort, sometimes I can't help but wonder if I'm not making it worse."

I turned. I couldn't help it. I turned and blatantly stared right at him.

I'd never heard of such a thing.

Didn't know it was even possible to visit another person's dreams.

And before I could ask to hear more, he looked and me and said, "Can I help you?"

Though the words might have seemed kind on the surface, believe me, that was hardly their intent, not in the least. The tone in his voice informed me loud and clear that he wasn't the least bit charmed by the sight of me, and was clearly annoyed by my eavesdropping.

"Um, sorry," I said, my eyes darting between him and his friend. "But I couldn't help but overhear, did you just say something about *entering someone's dream*?"

He narrowed his crinkly lids and looked me over carefully, as his friend, the one in the bright purple-and-orange Hawaiian shirt, the one he'd called Mort, decided to answer for him. "A dream visitation, that's right." He studied me carefully.

My mind swirled, spinning with all the major possibilities of such a thing, before saying, "And, um, could you maybe tell me how *someone* might go about doing something like that?" I pressed my lips together and prayed that didn't sound near as desperate to their ears as it had to mine.

They peered, scrutinized, practically dissected me in a

way that made it clear they were veering way closer toward *not* helping me, and I couldn't help but wonder if maybe my glow was at fault.

My pale green, barely there glow that, according to Bodhi anyway, clearly marked me as a member of the level 1.5 team—a virtual newbie as far as they were concerned.

Even though I hadn't had a chance to check it, to see if it'd been in anyway effected by everything I'd accomplished back in St. John, one look at the way they both glowed this soft, serene shade of yellow, well, I figured they probably thought that sort of information was way too advanced for someone as lowly as me.

I'd started to turn away, telling myself to just let it go since they were obviously reluctant to help, when Mort looked right at me, rubbed his chin with a set of surprisingly shiny, manicured nails, and said, "Well, first you gotta go to the place where all the dreams take place."

I swallowed and squinted, but otherwise did my best to remain still. Not wanting them to know that up until that moment, I'd had no idea there even was such a place.

Still, it was pretty clear by the look he exchanged with his friend that they both saw right through me.

Which is why I was so surprised when he ignored his friend's elbow nudging hard in his side as he said, "It's easy enough to find, all you have to do is—"

I leaned forward, eager to hear every last detail, only to have his words interrupted by someone shouting, "*Next!*"

I turned, seeing my number flash on the screen.

"Looks like it's your turn." Mort shrugged, along with his friend.

I was torn. Torn between wanting to check in on the earth plane, check in on my sister and friends, and my sudden but desperate need to learn more about the place where all the dreams happen.

I'd just started to broach it again when Mort's friend, the one who started all this, said, "Listen, you gonna take your turn or not?"

I glanced between the two of them, and it was clear by the way they both looked at me that neither one of them had any plans to tell me anything more than they already had.

But while the moment may have passed, the seed had been planted.

And as far as I was concerned, it was good enough for a start.

I thrust my ticket into Mort's hand and made a quick exit, hoping to find some kind of library or research center, some lofty place that might offer some answers, only to find Buttercup waiting right where I'd left him, with Bodhi, chomping hard on his straw, standing right alongside him.

"It's not what you think!" I screeched, regretting the words the instant they were out. I mean, *seriously*. It's not like I didn't know better. I was pretty well-versed in how that sort of denial never works.

"We've been summoned," Bodhi said, choosing to ignore my ridiculously transparent statement. "Which means you might want to take a quick moment to spruce yourself up. Oh, and you might also want to take a moment to hope *and* pray that no one finds out that the very first thing you did upon your return was come *here*."

I screwed up my face, annoyed by his words, but still, I did what he said. Ridding myself of what had become a pretty filthy swimsuit and cover-up, before manifesting a cool pair of jeans, some ballet flats, and a super cute T-shirt in its place.

"Better?" I lifted my brow and tilted my chin.

But Bodhi just grunted and rushed ahead, calling over his shoulder to say, "Whatever you do, just follow my lead, okay? *Please*. Just do yourself a favor and—"

He paused long enough for me to catch up.

"Do yourself a favor and let me handle everything."

He rounded a corner, and then another, then he led us up a whole lot of stairs to the same smoky-glass building where my life review had taken place.

And to be honest, if I'd had a stomach, that's pretty

much the exact moment it would've begun to spin and curl and somersault its way all the way down to my knees.

They were inside.

Aurora, Claude, Samson, Celia, and Royce—the entire Council assembled together, waiting to hear my side of things.

There was no way to avoid it.

I had no choice but to face it.

I'd acted willfully, rashly, stubbornly insisting on flaunting my freewill despite being warned not to.

No matter how well it might have turned out in the end, the fact was, it wasn't an assignment. If anything, it was the opposite. My guide had strictly forbidden it.

I squared my shoulders, checked my posture, and promised myself that whatever happened next, whatever happened on the other side of that door, I'd do everything I could to follow Bodhi's instructions and *not* make things any worse than they already were.

He looked at me and I nodded sagely in return, acting as though I was ready, even though I was pretty darn sure that I wasn't.

My hands trembling as he reached for the door, started to fling it wide open, only to have me slam my palm hard against it, slam it so I could get a better view of myself.

My eyes glued on my reflection, which was nothing *at all* like the last time I'd seen it.

Sure the usual sights were all there: blond hair, blue eyes, stubby nose, sunken chest—pretty much exactly the same as the last time I'd checked, but the glow that surrounded it was *entirely* different.

Okay, maybe I'm exaggerating.

Maybe it wasn't *entirely* different.

I mean, after all, it was still green.

But the *shade* of green was different. The *tone* of it was changed.

Like a seriously, noticeable, *marked* alteration.

The kind that can't be disputed.

"Congratulations." Bodhi nodded, flashing a quick smile my way. Though his face fell just as quickly, as he shook his head and said, "But before you get too carried away with yourself, you should know that there are consequences to our actions, as you're about to find out."

I nodded, aware of the words, noting the warning they contained, but still too entranced by my own reflection to really pay them much notice. Seeing the way the deeper, richer shade of green glowed and swirled all around me, and knowing it was the direct result of the choices I'd made.

"Remember what I told you," he said, his gaze signaling that he did not trust my ability not to say a word, not to blow it, to let him handle things—not for a moment.

I frowned, started to push past him, watching my glow wave and retreat as he stood to the side and ushered me in.

"In case you haven't noticed," I said, pausing to look at him, "I've totally got my glow on. So really, how bad can it be?"

I checked my reflection again, convinced that no matter what happened, no matter what the Council might say, my glow would be with me. It was something I'd earned. It wasn't going anywhere.

The thought instantly canceled by Bodhi's voice at my ear, saying, "Wrong again, Riley. Whatever the Council gives, they can also take away. And now, thanks to you, by the time we get out of here, we may never glow again."

author's note

While the characters and the situations they find themselves in are fictional, the story itself was loosely inspired by the 1733 slave revolt in the Danish West Indies (now known as St. John, U.S. Virgin Islands). In Africa, a number of noblemen and women, as well as wealthy merchants, had been sold into slavery after a revolt against them, then brought to the Caribbean to work as slaves. Eventually, they rebelled against the plantation owners and managers with the purpose of retaining other African slaves from different tribes to do their labor.

Purported to be among the first of those killed was a plantation owner and his young stepdaughter.

Also, the sadistic game of "beach bowling" is alleged to be true.

Questions for the Author

In what ways are you similar (or different) to Riley Bloom?

Actually, Riley and I share a lot in common. I know what it's like to be the baby of the family, and though I hate to admit it, I've also been known to hog the microphone while playing Rock Band on the Wii!

How do you come up with your characters?

Honestly, I'm not really sure! The story idea usually comes first, and then as I'm busy working on all the ins and outs of the new world I'm creating, the cast just sort of appears.

What was your inspiration for the "Here & Now," the magical realm where Riley lives?

Back when I first started working on The Immortals series, I did quite a bit of research on metaphysics, quantum physics, ghosts, spirits, and the afterlife, etc, all of which sort of fed into the concept of the "Here & Now." I guess, in a way, it's how I hope the afterlife will be.

Do you believe in ghosts?

In a word—yes. I've definitely experienced enough unexplainable phenomena to ever rule it out.

If a ghost tried to scare you with your own worst fears (the way the Radiant Boys try to scare Riley), what fears might they use against you?

I definitely drew upon all of my own worst fears while writing that scene—a crazy snake-haired clown wielding dental instruments is about as bad as it gets for me! The only thing missing was a really high ledge with no railing (I have a major fear of heights), but I wasn't sure how to fit that into the context, so I spared Riley that.

Did you grow up with an older sister the way Riley did? How many brothers and sisters do you have?

I have two older sisters, both of whom I completely idolized. There's a bit of an age gap between us, one is ten years older, and the other five years older, and trust me when I say that I did my best to emulate them. I listened to their music, watched their TV shows, and read their books—all of which was way more appealing than my own, more age-appropriate stuff. And like Riley, I used to try on their clothes and makeup when they were out with their friends, though I suspect that revelation will come as no surprise to them!

Where do you write your books?

I have a home office where I put in very, very long hours seven days a week—but I have the best job in the world, so I'm not complaining!

Have you always wanted to be a writer?

Well, first, I wanted to be a mermaid, and then a princess, but ever since sixth grade when I finished reading my first Judy Blume book, *Are You There, God? It's Me, Margaret*, I decided I'd rather write instead. I'd always been an avid reader, but Judy Blume's books were some of the first that I could directly relate to, and I knew then that someday I wanted to try to write like that too.

What would you do if you ever stopped writing?

Oh, I shudder to even think about it. I truly can't imagine a life without writing. Though I suppose I'd probably start traveling more. I've traveled a good bit already, both when I was working as a flight attendant and just on my own, but there are still so many places left to explore—oh, and I'd probably enroll in some art classes too—painting, jewelry making—crafty stuff like that.

What would your readers be most surprised to learn about you?

Not long ago, every time I finished writing a book I would celebrate by cleaning my house, which, I have to say, was sorely in need of it by then. But recently, I've come to realize just how very sad and pathetic that is, so now I get a pedicure instead (and save the housecleaning for another day)!

acknowledgments

Once again, great thanks are owed to Jean Feiwel, Matthew Shear, Rose Hilliard, Anne Marie Tallberg, Jennifer Doerr, Katy Hershberger, Brittney Kleinfelter, and Angela Goddard—just a few of the awesome, hardworking people who help bring my books to life; to Bill Contardi, for the wisdom and laughs; to Jeanette Harvey, who is, without a doubt, the best assistant I could ever imagine; to Sandy, for sharing the magic that is Oobleck; and of course, to my amazingly awesome readers—your enthusiasm and support mean the world to me!

DREAMLAND

A Riley Bloom Novel

ALL I WANTED, ALL I'D EVER DREAMED OF, WAS TO BE THIRTEEN. BUT THEN I DIED.

Riley Bloom's afterlife is about as good as it gets, except she'll never be a teenager. Riley desperately wants to speak to her older sister, Ever, to ask her advice. Ever is still alive and the only way Riley can reach her is to search for Dreamland – a place where ghosts can jump into dreams and talk to their loved ones. But when she finally gets there Riley discovers that Dreamland isn't as heavenly as it sounds. In fact, it's a total nightmare.

The third book in the witty, moving and heart-warming RILEY BLOOM series.

Turn the page to read an extract from Riley Bloom's next adventure . . .

I

The second I laid eyes on Aurora my shoulders slumped, my face unsquinched, and I heaved a deep sigh of relief knowing I had an ally, a friend on my side.

I was sure it would all be okay.

It was in the way her hair shimmered and shone—transforming from yellow to brown to black to red before starting the sequence all over again.

Her skin did the same, converting from the palest white to the darkest ebony, and every possible hue in between.

And her gown, her gorgeous yellow gown, sparkled and gleamed and swished at her feet like a crush of fallen stars.

Even though I no longer mistook her for an angel like I did the first time I saw her, still, the whole glistening sight calmed me in a major way.

But, as it turns out, I'd misread the whole thing.

As soon as I took one look at her aura—as soon as I

noted the way its usual bright popping purple had dimmed to a much duller violet—well, that's when I knew we were on opposite sides.

It was just like Bodhi had said: I had a heckuva lot to explain. My last Soul Catch hadn't exactly been assigned.

I stared at my feet, head hanging in shame, scraggly blond hair hanging limply before me as I forced myself to shuffle behind him. Using those last remaining moments to run a frantic search through my best, most plausible excuses—mentally rehearsing my story again and again like a panicky actor on opening night.

Even though I'd only been doing my job as a Soul Catcher when I coaxed and convinced a whole lot of ghosts to cross the bridge to where they belonged, there was no denying the fact that I'd been told to look the other way—to mind my own business. To not get involved by sticking my semi-stubby nose in places where it most certainly didn't belong.

But did I listen?

Uh, not exactly.

Instead I charged full speed ahead into a whole heap of trouble.

I followed Bodhi to the stage, his back so stiff and his hands so clenched I was glad I couldn't see his face. Though, if I had to guess, I'd be willing to bet that his mouth, free of the straw he usually chomped when the Council wasn't around, was pinched into a thin, grim line, while his green eyes, heavily shadowed by his insanely thick fringe of lashes, were sparking and flaring as he thought of ways to rid himself of me once and for all.

I peered under my bangs, watching as Aurora took her place next to Claude, who sat next to Samson, who was right beside Celia, who was so tiny and petite she was able to share an armrest with Royce without either one of them having to compromise or fight for equal space. And seeing them all assembled like that, waiting to hear just how I might go about explaining myself, well, that's when I remembered the most important evidence of all.

The one undeniable thing that required no verbal explanation, as it was right there smack dab in the front and center, visible for all to see.

I had my glow on.

Actually, scratch that. It wasn't just my usual glow. It was far more impressive than that.

As a reward for all I'd accomplished my glow had significantly deepened. Going from what started out as a barely there, pale green shimmer straight into a . . . well . . .a somewhat deeper green shimmer.

Okay, maybe the change wasn't all that drastic, but the thing is, what it lacked in drama it made up for in substance.

Let's just say that it couldn't be missed.

After all, I'd seen it.

Bodhi had seen it.

Even Buttercup had looked right at me and barked a few times as he wagged his tail and spun around.

All of which I took as a pretty good sign that the Council would see it too—from what I knew of them, they didn't miss a thing.

I relaxed, pushed my hair off my face, and thought: *How bad can it be when my glow is so clearly minty green?*

But then I remembered what Bodhi had said about consequences and actions—about the Council's ability to give and take at will. Insisting that because of my failure to follow orders, it was really quite possible that by the time we were done, neither of us would ever glow again.

Knowing I had to act fast, do whatever it took to get them to see my side of things, I charged straight ahead.

I had no time for trouble. No time to waste.

Just moments before I'd learned something extraordinary—had heard about some mysterious dimension where all the dreams take place—and I was determined to find it.

Besides, I was pretty sure Bodhi couldn't be trusted. The fact that he found me a burden wasn't a secret.

When it came right down to it, it was every man, er,

make that *ghost,* for himself. So I squeezed him right out and took center stage.

He gasped in astonishment. Tried to push me away. But he was too late, and I was too fast, and before he could do anything more, I was already standing smack dab in front of the Council, pushing aside any lingering fear.

Fear was for sissies. Of that I was sure.

It was time for me to tell them my side of things.

My story. My way.

And I was just about to begin, when I noticed the way Aurora's aura grew dimmer, as the rest of the Council's followed suit. Darkening in a way that made my mouth grow so dry, and my throat go so lumpy, the words jammed in my throat.

I stood shaking. Mute. Watching as Bodhi—my guide—the one person whose job it was to help me—shook his head and smirked. Leaving no doubt in my mind just how much he'd enjoy watching me burn.

2

The next thing I knew, Bodhi had leaped right before me, and said, "Hi!"

Chasing it with a dazzling smile—one that showcased his dimples and made his eyes gleam. And as if that weren't enough, he then shifted in a way that shamelessly allowed a chunk of wavy brown hair to fall into those eyes and tangle with his extra thick lashes—just so he could sweep his bangs off his face and smile again.

It was a Hollywood move.

Slick.

Superficial.

Spurious (thank you word-a-day calendar!) in the very worst way.

The kind of move that either makes your heart flutter, or makes you go *blech*. And seeing Bodhi do it, well, it just made me feel weird.

But when the move didn't win him the reaction he'd hoped, when the members of the Council didn't swoon all over themselves, he shifted gears, cleared his voice, and looking directly at them, uttered a very serious-sounding, "Hello."

To be honest, I was a little embarrassed by the double greeting, but before I could do anything to stop him he said, "As you know, Riley, Buttercup, and I ran into a little trouble recently, and . . ."

He rambled.

Oh boy, did he ramble.

He rambled in a way that was nothing but a bunch of bippidy blah blah to my ears.

Rambled in a way that made my head go all dizzy and squeezy.

Rambled in a way that wasn't the least bit effective—or at least not where the Council was concerned. And I knew I had to stop him before it got any worse. So the second he paused, I jumped in to say, "I think what Bodhi means is . . ."

He swung toward me, glaring in a way that was half rage, half horrified disbelief. But it wasn't enough to stop me. Not even close.

But before I could even get started, Royce, with the dark wavy hair, smooth dark skin, and glinting green eyes that amounted to the kind of breath-stealing good looks usually reserved for movie screens, said, "That's enough, Riley."

I froze—too afraid to look at Bodhi—too afraid to look at anyone—those three simple words stopping me cold. Not once in my ridiculously brief twelve years of life had I heard that phrase used for anything other than to stop me from some type of behavior an adult found extremely annoying.

An awkward pause followed, broken by Celia, who stood beside Royce, her usual cornflower blue glow once again beaming at full force when she said, "There is no need to continue. No need to make excuses or explain. We have seen everything."

I nodded. Gulped. It was all I could do.

My eyes locking on Samson's deep violet ones as his hands clasped either side of his seat. "You acted on your own. You acted willfully, wildly, you ignored Bodhi's instructions, and put yourselves in great danger." He rose to his feet and stood rigid before me. "In the future we ask that you consult with us first before you go off on your own. No matter where you find yourself on the earth plane, you must never forget that we are but one telepathic message away."

He shot me a stern look, Bodhi too, the two of us frozen, unsure what to do, when Aurora said, "There is no need to fear us. We are here to offer guidance, support, and assistance if you find that you need it. And while I know you are eager to advance, you must trust that each and every assignment has been carefully selected to match your level of progress." Her gaze locked on mine, making sure I understood, before she went on to add, "That said, you have still managed to succeed where many other Soul Catchers have failed. Congratulations."

Bodhi softened, as a whistle of air I didn't even know I'd been holding escaped from my lips. And when I glanced down at Buttercup, I watched as he raised his rump high and let loose in a flurry of wiggles—an overdose of cuteness I found myself wishing he'd stop.

There was no need to overdo it. Not when I'd just been acknowledged—no, scratch that—not when I'd just been *congratulated* by Aurora, who I was pretty sure was the Council's queen bee.

I'd put myself in danger. I'd taken great risks. I'd done the exact opposite of what Bodhi had ordered—and look where it got me:

Glowing before the Council.

Graciously accepting great praise.

Congratulations!

The word spun through my head.

I wasn't in trouble. All was okay. Actually, it was better than okay. Once again, I'd succeeded where others had failed.

I knew it.

The Council knew it.

And my glow proved it.

It was Bodhi who needed the attitude adjustment. Me—I was at the top of my game.

I reveled in my success, reliving the praise over and over again.

My thoughts interrupted by the melodic lilt of Aurora's voice when she added, "It is obvious that you are in need of greater challenges in the future, so we will do our best to provide them for you."

I nodded, arranging my face into the perfect expression of humility, saving the victory dance for later.

My attention soon stolen by Claude, whose long, slim fingers fiddled with the scraggly beard that stopped just shy of his waist, as he said, "And so, in light of all that you have accomplished, we agree that you two are in need of a break."

I glanced at Bodhi, taking a sidelong peek at the brand-spanking-new sneakers I was sure he'd manifested just for this meeting, the dark denim jeans that pooled around his ankles in that cool-guy way, his slouchy blue sweater that skimmed his lean form, making my way up to his ridiculously cute face which, just the sight of it alone, caused my throat to go all lumpy and hot as an unexpected wave of nostalgia for all that we'd shared threatened to swallow me whole.

As much as I'd longed for a new guide (pretty much since the moment Bodhi and I met), just when I was about to get one, well, I could hardly believe our days of Soul Catching together were coming to such a quick end. After this meeting, we might never see each other again.

For some strange reason, the thought didn't spark the kind of joy I would've expected. If anything, it did just the opposite. It made me feel all twisty and turvy and a little bit empty.

But, as it turns out, I was wrong.

Dead wrong.

The Council had other ideas.

"Take a break from Soul Catching," Aurora said, nodding in a way that made her hair dance and swirl. "Take some time to relax and enjoy yourselves."

My face squinched, unsure how to take that.

I mean, hadn't I just been congratulated?

And didn't that sort of praise mean I could skip a few grades and move on to the kind of big, scary ghosts the experienced Soul Catchers dealt with?

It was Celia who set me straight. "While we are all quite delighted with your performance, Riley, and while it's clear that we'll need to find greater challenges for you, we think you could use some time off." Her tiny hands fluttered at her waist like a hummingbird before a feeder. "And once you're sufficiently refreshed, we'll happily send you and Bodhi on your next assignment. We are delighted with the way you two work together. Clearly you bring out the best in each other."

I gaped. And I'm talkin' the bug-eyed, jaw-to-the-knees kind of gaped. I mean, seriously? *Bring out the best in each other?* Was she kidding? Had any of them actually reviewed the footage of Bodhi and me attempting to work together?

All we did was fight!

And argue.

And willfully oppose each other every chance that we got.

The only times we ever pitched in, rolled up our sleeves, and put our vast and varied differences aside, was after things were so far gone we had no other choice but to rely on each other.

But apparently that wasn't all. Oh, no, they were a long way from done, because right as I was still reeling from that, Royce piped in and said, "While we take some time in choosing your next assignment, you and Bodhi, and yes, even you, Buttercup—" Royce's eyes sparkled when Buttercup, upon hearing his name, licked his chops and wiggled his rump once again. "—you should all enjoy your time off. Spend some time with family. Visit with friends. The important thing is for you to rest up and recharge. Don't worry, we'll find you when it's time for your next assignment. But for now, you are released."

Released.

Freed.

Undeniably dismissed.

And yet, even though I'd heard every word, all I could do was just stand there and gawk, watching as Bodhi and Buttercup shot across the stage and made a mad dash for the door. Suddenly paralyzed by the horrible realization that, unlike me, they had other, better places to be.

The Council had vanished—just *poof* and they were gone. And knowing it was lame (not to mention pathetic) to keep standing there long after everyone else had vacated, I hung my head low and retraced Bodhi's and Buttercup's steps.

The dismal truth of my existence blooming before me: While I may have excelled at Soul Catching, I was a total failure when it came to having an afterlife.

My social life was even deader than I.

I had no friends. No hobbies. No place to go other than my own room.

And while it's true that my parents and grandparents were Here, it's also true that they were busy with their own afterlives.

The Here & Now was nothing like the earth plane. I

didn't need anyone to pay my bills, prepare my meals, sign permission slips, drive me around, or just generally look after me in a shelter-food-and-money kind of way. Everything I could possibly want, and/or need, could be had simply by wishing it—which meant that other than dropping by to check in and say hi, my family was no longer responsible for me.

They'd moved on.

And the pathetic truth was, from what I'd seen, my grandparents were way more popular than I.

I slammed through the door and hurled myself outside, determined to do whatever it took to get myself an afterlife.

A selected list of titles available from Macmillan Children's Books

The prices shown below are correct at the time of going to press. However, Macmillan Publishers reserves the right to show new retail prices on covers, which may differ from those previously advertised.

Alyson Noël

Also by Alyson Noël – for older readers

All Pan Macmillan titles can be ordered from our website, www.panmacmillan.com, or from your local bookshop and are also available by post from:

Bookpost, PO Box 29, Douglas, Isle of Man IM99 1BQ

Credit cards accepted. For details:
Telephone: 01624 677237
Fax: 01624 670923
Email: bookshop@enterprise.net
www.bookpost.co.uk

Free postage and packing in the United Kingdom